The Real People
Book Three

THE WHITE PATH

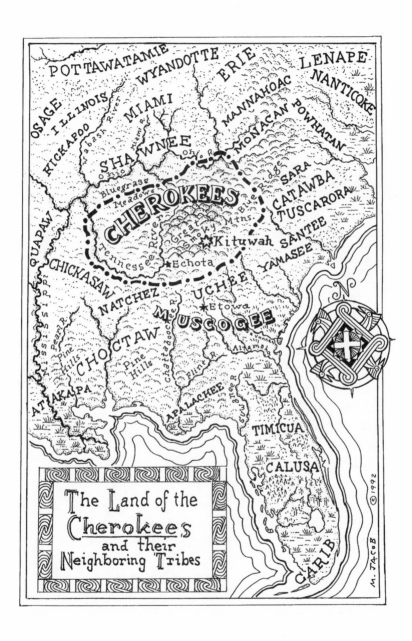

The Land of the
Cherokees
and their
Neighboring Tribes

ROBERT J. CONLEY

The White Path

A Double D Western
D O U B L E D A Y
New York   London   Toronto   Sydney   Auckland

West

A Double D Western
PUBLISHED BY DOUBLEDAY
a division of Bantam Doubleday Dell Publishing Group, Inc.
1540 Broadway, New York, New York 10036

Double D Western, Doubleday,
and the portrayal of the letters DD
are trademarks of Doubleday, a division of
Bantam Doubleday Dell Publishing Group, Inc.

All of the characters in this book are fictitious,
and any resemblance to actual persons, living or
dead, is purely coincidental.

Map and illustrations by Murv Jacob

Library of Congress Cataloging-in-Publication Data

Conley, Robert J.
The white path / Robert J. Conley.—1st ed.
    p.   cm.—(The Real people; bk. 3) (A Double D western)
1. Cherokee Indians—Fiction. I. Title. II. Series: Conley, Robert J. Real
people; bk. 3.
PS353.0494W47   1993
813'.54—dc20   92-39504
                         CIP

ISBN 0-385-41934-1
Copyright © 1993 by Robert J. Conley
All Rights Reserved
Printed in the United States of America
July 1993
First Edition

10   9   8   7   6   5   4   3   2   1

THE WHITE PATH

One

LIKE-A-PUMPKIN had been spared the recent violence, yet he still felt uneasy. He felt as if he were living on borrowed time. He had arrived back at Men's Town in his homeland, the country of the Real People, following a long absence. He had stumbled unsuspecting into the immediate aftermath of a violent revolution, and some had rushed at him to kill him, but Edohi had stopped them.

"There's been enough killing," Edohi had said, and the people had listened to Edohi. So the revolution was over, and it had been a revolution in every sense of the word. Over the years, the *Ani-Kutani*, the ancient priesthood, had evolved into a powerful, absolute ruling class over all of the vast domain of the Real People. They had ruled by fear, not so much fear of violence or force or even numbers, but fear of powerful spiritual forces, which they alone were said to be able to control.

But at last they had gone too far, and in spite of the

fears, Edohi had led an army of Real People, mostly from his own town of Ijodi, in an attack on Men's Town, the seat of the priestly government. They had killed all of the priests, all who had been there to be killed. Like-a-Pumpkin, who had been sent west with two other priests in search of the house of Thunder to bring back the rain, had arrived back home just after the big fight, and he had been spared.

And there was another one who might still be among the living somewhere. Like-a-Pumpkin had told the people of how he and his traveling companions had been captured and enslaved by a band of fierce people in the West, people with strange ways and a strange language. Water Moccasin had been killed trying to escape. Later Like-a-Pumpkin had managed to escape, but the third priest, Deadwood Lighter, was, as far as Like-a-Pumpkin knew, still a slave to the fierce people. Therefore, he and Like-a-Pumpkin were the only two surviving priests.

It had been a violent revolution which had successfully overthrown an oppressive government. But the *Ani-Kutani* had been much more than a government. The Real People lived lives of precarious balance in a world which existed between two other worlds, two worlds of powerfully opposed spiritual forces. Any wrong move could result in disaster. The *Ani-Kutani* prevented disaster by prescribing rules of behavior for everyone and by conducting public rituals and ceremonies designed to maintain balance and harmony. Some of the people believed firmly that because the priests had been killed, the world would soon come to an end. The revolution, they thought, had been a form of mass suicide.

Without the *Ani-Kutani*, each of the towns of the Real

People was on its own, completely autonomous. No more was there any central authority, and, therefore, there were many who suddenly recognized no authority, and so the reigning authority had become chaos. Town bullies had become town leaders. In spite of the fact that spokeswomen for each of the seven matrilineal clans had sworn that there would be no attempts at clan revenge following the killing of the priests, such retaliation had become commonplace. And the popularity of the conjurers had burgeoned. People flocked to them for protection from both known and imagined dangers, dangers both physical and spiritual.

And there were some who recalled with dread the final words of the head *Kutani*, Standing-in-the-Doorway, as he stood at the edge of the temple mound in Men's Town, his robes ablaze.

"It's the end of the world," he had shouted, and some had come to wonder if he had not made an accurate prediction.

In Ijodi, even the leaders of the revolution, Edohi, Hemp Carrier, the Spoiler, even these were anxious about the future of the Real People. But there was one at least among the Real People who was more than content with the way in which things had developed. In Kituwah, the boy Gnat had been given back his uncle.

But Like-a-Pumpkin knew that there were people who still thought that he should be killed. He was the last *Kutani*. Well, there was poor Deadwood Lighter somewhere out west probably still living in miserable slavery with those vile, fierce people. But Like-a-Pumpkin was the last *Kutani* as far as anyone knew. He was the last

Kutani alive and at home. And constantly he wondered just how much longer he would remain alive.

Then there was the rain. The rain had come just behind Like-a-Pumpkin, and of course, the reason he and the other two priests had been sent to the West in the first place had been to bring back the rain. Many people believed that he had done that. That was one reason, he thought, that he had not been killed. But others explained the rain in other ways. Some said that the blood of all the slain *Ani-Kutani* had brought the rain, and some even dared to say that Standing-in-the-Doorway had been right all along, that his killing of the young woman, Edohi's wife, Corn Flower, at the big ceremony had worked, and that Edohi and the others had been impatient and had not waited long enough. Some few maintained that old Gone-in-the-Water, the conjurer from Ijodi, had brought the rain by working some secret magic.

Like-a-Pumpkin had gone back home to Kituwah, and he had tried to be quiet and unobtrusive. That, he had decided, was the most likely way to stay alive for a while. Of course, Gnat was thrilled at that turn of events. Not only had his favorite uncle returned from the far West, but he had actually returned to Kituwah, not to Men's Town. He was home. And when Like-a-Pumpkin had been at home again for a little while, long enough to feel a little more comfortable, he realized that he was the keeper of a most important secret. All of the *Ani-Kutani* who had remained at home were dead. He and possibly Deadwood Lighter were the only ones left alive. Deadwood Lighter had not been a scribe, and that meant that Like-a-Pumpkin was the only living being who could write the old writing, the sacred writing. He was afraid to let that be

known lest that little secret incite someone to more violence, yet he hated to think that his death would one day
mean the absolute and total loss of the writing.

So Like-a-Pumpkin took Gnat with him out of the
town of Kituwah, away from any listening ears and watching eyes. For a time they only walked and talked, and they
talked of nothing in particular. But at last, Like-a-Pumpkin sat down on a knoll with his nephew to rest. The knoll
was in an open area, so that no one could come close
without being seen. Like-a-Pumpkin looked at the boy
there beside him. He was very young, approaching nine
years, to have a heavy burden placed on his shoulders. But
Like-a-Pumpkin could think of no other way.

"Nephew," he said, "you know, of course, that I was a
priest."

"Of course, Uncle," said Gnat.

"And you know that if I had not been away when the
big fight came, they would have killed me there at Men's
Town along with the others."

Gnat ducked his head and looked at the ground between his knees.

"Yes," he said.

"So you know, then, that I must be very careful what I
say or do. It would be very easy for someone to become
angry and decide that I should be dead with the others."

"They wouldn't do that, Uncle," protested Gnat, des-
peration showing on his face and in his voice. "Not now.
Would they?"

"Don't be afraid for me," said Like-a-Pumpkin. "I'm
not trying to frighten you. I just want to be sure that you
understand I'm in a very precarious position. I have to be
careful. Do you understand that?"

"Yes, Uncle," said Gnat.

"Good. Because now I want to tell you something. Something very important."

Gnat's eyes opened wide, and he listened with all of his attention while his uncle proceeded.

"I have inside me a great secret. It's a very important thing, but it's also a dangerous thing. I don't want this secret to be lost when I die. It's too important a thing to be lost. Can I tell it to you?"

"Yes," said Gnat.

"You can never tell anyone else. You'll have to keep the secret, just as I do, and someday, very carefully, pass it along to someone else, to some young boy you trust to do the same. Learn it, keep it and pass it on. Do you understand?"

"I think so."

"You can't tell anyone, not your mother or your father. No one."

"I'll never tell," said Gnat, "and neither will the boy I choose to tell it to someday. I'll see to that."

"Someday perhaps, when the Real People have forgotten the *Ani-Kutani*, when there is no one alive who remembers them, then perhaps the one with the secret can let it be known again. But that will not be me or you."

"What is this secret, Uncle?"

"It is a way to write our language."

"To what?"

"To put down marks that we can read. I'll show you."

Like-a-Pumpkin picked up a stick and drew a figure in the dirt.

"Remember this," he said. "Every time you see it, you say the sound of 'ee.' "

Gnat looked at the strange symbol there on the ground.
" 'Eee,' " he said.

Then Like-a-Pumpkin drew another.

"This one says 'ya,' " he said.

"Ee-ya," said Gnat.

"Yes," said Like-a-Pumpkin. "Iya."

He scratched once more the first symbol, and then two
new ones. And he gave the values of the new ones to his
nephew. Gnat tried to put them all together.

"Iya-Iyusti," he read. "It makes your name."

"Yes, Nephew. And there are many more signs to learn.
It will take some time, but when you've learned them all,
you will be able to write down anything you can say. And
I will be able to read it. Or if I write down something, you
will be able to read it."

Then Like-a-Pumpkin rubbed out the marks in the
dirt.

"And every time you practice," he said, "you must wipe
it out. Never practice where anyone can see you, but find
a way to practice every day. It won't be easy when you
have to be so secretive. Just always remember, the survival
of the writing will depend on you."

So Like-a-Pumpkin found a way to pass his knowledge
on, and in his nephew Gnat, he found a willing and an
eager pupil. Every day they walked together out of the
village, and every day they practiced, and Gnat each day
learned new symbols until he knew them all. And Like-a-
Pumpkin was proud of his nephew, but he was still afraid.

Another major event occurred in the life of Like-a-Pumpkin shortly after his return home. At first no one seemed
interested in his adventures. They were all too busy revel-

ing in their own recent success or worrying about the impending doom they had almost certainly brought down upon themselves. But as more time went by, they began to get curious about Like-a-Pumpkin and his two comrades. Where had they been, and what had happened to them?

He was in his sister's house in Kituwah when the people came that day.

"Like-a-Pumpkin," he heard someone shout. "Come out. We want to talk with you."

His first thought was that they had come to kill him. He considered trying to flee, but there was no way out except through them. There was no place to go. He resigned himself to his fate. If they meant to kill him, well, he would show them that he knew how to die. He stepped boldly outside to face them, but inside his own body, he was trembling with fear.

"Like-a-Pumpkin," said one of the men, "when you went away, there were three of you."

"Yes," said Like-a-Pumpkin. "Water Moccasin and Deadwood Lighter were my two companions."

"And why did they not return with you?"

"We were captured by some fierce people far to the west," said Like-a-Pumpkin. "They made us slaves. One day, Water Moccasin ran, and they shot an arrow in his back and killed him. Deadwood Lighter and I were separated. I don't know what became of him, but one day I saw my chance, and I escaped."

"How did you manage it?" one asked.

"I thought about the story of rabbit's escape from the wolves," said Like-a-Pumpkin, "and I imitated him. I sang the rabbit song, and I danced as I was picking up wood. My 'master' watched me with curiosity, and he followed me farther and farther into the woods. At last I clubbed him with a stick, and then I stabbed him with his own knife, and I ran away."

They asked for more details. They wanted him to describe the fierce people, and again and again, they asked him to tell about the escape, the rabbit song and dance. And when Like-a-Pumpkin realized that they were enjoying his story and that they did not intend to kill him, he too began to enjoy it. He sang the song and he danced the dance as he told the tale, and his audience laughed and applauded and asked him to tell it again. Then one day, they gave him a new name. It was a warrior's name, because it was given to him as a result of his deeds against an enemy, and the fact that none of the Real People knew this enemy made little difference. It was a great honor, and for the first time in his life, he did not feel little and funny and insignificant. They looked up to him. They respected him. And his new name was Dancing Rabbit.

Two

OUTSIDE OF IJODI, Edohi sat on the high hill-top overlooking the town to his right and the road to his left. For a short while after the destruction of Men's Town and the killing of the priests, he had been elated, for he had been the chosen war leader of that successful rebellion. But time had taken its toll, and Edohi had begun to think, not of his great success, but of the terrible loss of his wife and his resulting loneliness. He also thought about the slaughter itself. Bloody images of the assault on Men's Town came back into his mind more and more often. They even haunted his sleep. And over and over again he saw the image of the final moments of that awful head *Kutani*, saw Standing-in-the-Doorway there before the temple, on the mound, his robes aflame, saw the face distorted in agony and terror, heard the final, frightening prophecy of the priest.

"It's the end of the world."

And all of these images, all of these memories, combined with the current events throughout the country of the Real People in the mind of Edohi, and they caused him to dread the future. He had begun to wonder if the *Ani-Kutani* had been right all along, and he was beginning to shoulder a tremendous burden of guilt. He wondered if he had indeed brought about the beginning of the end.

Women were fighting with each other over ownership of the garden plots and over division of the produce from the community gardens. They fought also over the division of labor in those community fields. Everywhere people were surly or argumentative. Men still went out to hunt, but often they fought with each other over the rights to hunt in certain areas of the forests.

Edohi tried to remind himself of the abuses of the *Ani-Kutani*, but the severity of those abuses seemed to diminish with the passage of time and by comparison with the current rampant anarchy. It seemed to Edohi that perhaps the tyranny of the *Ani-Kutani* was preferable to the total lack of authority that had followed.

And there were the pressures of his family and the family of his late wife. They all thought that he should marry again. And there was a wife just waiting for him to make his decision. Edohi's wife, Corn Flower, had a younger and unwed sister, Sohi, Hickory Nut. It would be right and natural, they all said, for Edohi to take Sohi as his wife. But the end of the world was at hand, and Edohi was not in a mood to marry.

So, as before, he stayed away as much as he could. He avoided all people as much as possible, but especially he avoided his family and his in-laws. And most especially he avoided the young and beautiful Sohi.

He sat on the large rock there on the top of the hill,

and he looked out over the valley, looking at nothing in particular, and he brooded over all these things, and he was alone in the quiet of the lonely mountaintop. Then he was startled by a voice which came from close behind him.

"Edohi," it said, and it was soft and low.

Edohi flinched, startled by the suddenness and the closeness of the voice, and then he turned to look, and he saw the withered old man standing there.

"How did you get up here?" said Edohi.

"How did you get up here?" said Gone-in-the-Water.

"But I didn't hear anything."

"Neither did I."

Edohi was exasperated with the old conjurer. He had not wanted company, and he was a little embarrassed at having been surprised so. He also wondered at Gone-in-the-Water's physical stamina. He would not have thought the old man capable anymore of climbing the mountain.

"Why are you here?" he asked, trying, none too successfully, to conceal his irritation.

"I came to see you, Edohi."

"Why, old man?"

"Don't you know? Do you have eyes? Ears? But perhaps you don't know. You bring your eyes and ears up here where they can't see or hear anything except the birds and the four-legged creatures that scamper around up here with you. Are you joining the four-footed tribes? Have you abandoned your people?"

"I don't know what you're talking about, old man," said Edohi, and he turned his back once again to look out over the valley and to hide his own face from Gone-in-the-Water.

"Edohi," said Gone-in-the-Water, "you were chosen."
Edohi turned suddenly and fiercely on the conjurer.

"Yes," he said. "You told me that before, and I led the fight. I killed all the priests and burned Men's Town. I did that because you said that I had been chosen. But chosen for what? Look around us. Yes, I have eyes and ears, and I have seen and heard what is happening all over our land. Have I brought about the end of the world, old man? Is that what I was chosen for?"

Gone-in-the-Water sat down on the rock with a heavy sigh, and Edohi thought that the conjurer looked very old and very weak. He felt a little guilty for having spoken so sharply to one so old and venerable.

"Sit down, Edohi," said Gone-in-the-Water, and Edohi sat on the ground there in front of the old man, and the old man began to tell a tale.

"A long time ago a few of our young men went on a journey to see what they could see. They went a long way from home, far away from the country of the Real People, and eventually they came to a place where people called Tsundigewi lived.

"These Tsundigewi were little people. They stood up only as high as the knees of the Real People, and they had no houses. They lived in nests scooped out of the sand. The Real People learned to talk to these little people, and they learned that these pitiful little people lived in constant fear. Wild geese and other birds came in flocks from the south to make war on them, and the birds carried them away in great numbers each time they attacked.

"The Real People asked the Tsundigewi why they did not defend themselves against the birds, but the little people said they did not know how. So the Real People taught them how to make warclubs and how to use them. They decided also to teach the little men how to make bows and arrows, but before they had time to do that, the geese came, a great flock that darkened the sky.

"The little people ran in terror to their nests, but the geese followed them and plucked them out with their beaks and ate them. But the Real People and the little people with their new clubs knocked the geese in their heads until they had killed enough to drive the rest of them away.

"The little people rejoiced. They gave a big feast and dance, and they thanked the Real People for having saved their lives. At last these young men, the Real People, decided that they had been away from home long enough. They said goodbye to the little people and returned to their own homes."

Gone-in-the-Water paused in his tale. "Those little people," he said, "are like our people, and the *Ani-Kutani* were the geese. You were like the young men who came to visit the little people and saved them from the geese. Do you understand my story?"

"Yes," said Edohi, "but—"

"The story isn't over yet," said Gone-in-the-Water. "Our young men forgot something. Do you know what they forgot?"

"No," said Edohi. "Yes. Wait. Of course. They forgot to teach the little people how to make bows and arrows, but they had already driven off the geese, and the little people knew how to defend themselves if the geese should come back again."

"Listen to the rest of the story," said the old man.

"When the men from the Real People were gone, and

the little people were alone once more, they were attacked again, but this time they were attacked by large sandhill cranes, and the little people were so short that they could not reach the heads of the cranes to hit them with their clubs. The big birds plucked all of the little people out of their nests and ate them, and now the Tsundigewi are no more."

The story was over, and Edohi sat and stared at the ground in front of him. Gone-in-the-Water sat silently for a long time. Edohi wondered if the old man would ever speak again. At last, he himself broke the silence.

"Uncle," he said, "I think I know what you are telling me. The young men saved the little people from one danger, but they gave up too soon. They went away and left the little people to face an even greater danger. They should have stayed longer. They should have anticipated the greater danger and prepared the little people for it as well."

Gone-in-the-Water slowly nodded his head.

"If the *Ani-Kutani* were like the wild geese," Edohi continued, "the present craziness all around us is like the sandhill cranes, and if I quit now, the people will be destroyed."

"Ah," said Gone-in-the-Water, "so you are still capable of understanding. I'm glad of that. I was afraid that your brain had stopped working right."

"I understand you, Uncle," said Edohi, "but how do I fight this present situation? There are no priests to kill. The Real People are their own enemies this time. How do we fight ourselves?"

"The first step is to make up your mind that you are going to do it, that you are not going to give up, that you are not going to pull in your head like the turtle and stay in there."

"The way I've been doing," said Edohi. "I understand you. I'll come out, Uncle. I'll do what I can, but I need help. I need your guidance. I really have no idea what to do this time."

"Edohi," said Gone-in-the-Water, "what was the enemy the time you led the fight?"

"Why, the *Ani-Kutani.*"

"Yes. Of course. But what was the job of the *Ani-Kutani?*"

"Well," said Edohi, "it was to perform the ceremonies, I guess."

"Then the ceremonies were not the enemy?"

"No. I don't think so."

"What is the purpose of the ceremonies?"

"To keep us in balance here on this earth."

"The purpose of the ceremonies is to keep all things in balance," said Gone-in-the-Water. "Have you ever seen our world so out of balance?"

"No," said Edohi. "I have not."

"Then what do you suppose we need?"

"Of course," said Edohi. "We need our ceremonies. But who can conduct the ceremonies? We killed all the priests."

"There is one you spared," said the conjurer.

"Like-a-Pumpkin."

"He is now called Dancing Rabbit," said Gone-in-the-Water. "But you must take care in approaching him. He'll be afraid for his life, with good reason. Having killed the priests, the people will be suspicious of the last priest if he begins to try to lead the ceremonies again. Go to him. Talk to him. Seek his advice."

"I will," said Edohi. "And thank you, Uncle, for bringing me once again out of my shell."

"Ah," said Gone-in-the-Water, "what else is an old man good for?"

They walked together down the mountainside, and Edohi walked with Gone-in-the-Water to his tiny house on the edge of town, outside the walls. The old man headed for the low doorway of his hovel, and Edohi turned to walk in a direction away from Ijodi.

"You're not going home?" said the old man.

"No, Uncle," said Edohi, "I'm going to Kituwah to find Dancing Rabbit."

"Ah, good," said Gone-in-the-Water. "I wish you success."

He stood there in front of his house and watched until Edohi had disappeared down the road. Then he bent over and stepped inside. There was a crash in the far corner. He jumped and looked, and then he saw there the shards of a pot that had been sitting on a low shelf on the wall.

"Noisy," he shouted angrily. "You clumsy little turd. Why are you messing with my things when I'm away from home? Look what you've done. You've broken it. And where is your wretched little partner, huh? Where's Ugly? Where is he hiding? He's probably up to no good, just like you are. Find him and run along with you both. Go out in the woods to do your mischief. Go on."

A few miles away, outside of Kituwah, Dancing Rabbit sat with his nephew Gnat in a secluded spot. They did not talk. They drew signs in the dirt, and in this way, they were carrying on a complete conversation. Gnat was proud, for he had always admired his uncle, and now he shared with him a secret of tremendous importance. Dancing Rabbit was proud, because his nephew had proved himself to be bright and quick and dependable. The writing would survive.

Three

THE TIME immediately following the killing of the priests had been for many a time for the changing of names, and one of those who received a new name was the Shawnee captive who had been the Spoiler's slave. She had freed him when he had saved her youngest daughter, Sohi, from the rattlesnake, and he had stayed around. He had followed her and continued to serve her like a faithful dog. He had wooed her, and at last, she had accepted him. And he had fought alongside the Real People against the priests. And so the Real People, especially those who lived in Ijodi, had decided that this man was no longer an outcast. He had been adopted by the Bird People, Edohi's own clan, and he had therefore become one of the Real People. They began to call him simply Sawahani, Shawnee.

Shawnee had spent most of a day deep in the woods on a hunt, and toward the end of the day, he returned to Ijodi. He was anxious, as always, to get back to the house of his new wife, the Cherokee woman warrior known as the Spoiler. In the mind of Shawnee, the Spoiler was the finest, the most admirable woman he had ever seen, and he could scarcely believe his own good fortune, and the strange turn of events in his life that had led him to her. He was worried about his wife's people, yet still his heart was light as he approached the Spoiler's house. Chaos might swirl around them, but in that house between those two people was perfect harmony. The Spoiler's house was Shawnee's house of refuge.

Shawnee knew that the Spoiler wanted a new bear rug, and they always needed meat, and so he had gone out to kill a bear. And he was returning home successful. He had the bear, a small, male black bear, draped over his shoulders. In front of his wife's house, he dropped the carcass to the ground. The Spoiler had heard his approach, and she stepped out the door just as he was straightening up again.

"Ah," she said, "a good one. That will make several meals."

Her new husband was a good provider, and she was proud of him. She often wondered at the fact that she could be so happy with a Shawnee man, a people for whom she had once had nothing but bitter hatred.

"Yes," he said, "and a nice rug for your floor."

"I'll get busy and prepare it right away," she said, ducking to go back through her door for her tools. Shawnee sat down on the ground and leaned back against the house. He was tired from carrying the bear the long way home. The Spoiler re-emerged a moment later with a knife and a scraper in her hands. She bent over the carcass of the bear and began slicing through the skin expertly.

"You were gone a long time," she said. "Did you have trouble finding this one?"

"I went far out," said Shawnee. "I wanted to avoid any problems with hunters who claimed the rights to the land close by. Even so, as I was returning, I was met by All Bones. He tried to claim this bear. He said that I had killed it in his area. We argued for a while, but I finally convinced him that I had killed the bear somewhere else, and I was only passing through his territory to return home."

"Where did you encounter All Bones?" asked the Spoiler, looking up for a moment from her work.

"Just north of town," said Shawnee, "not far out."

"That region doesn't belong to him," she said with a frown. "It doesn't belong to anyone."

"I didn't challenge him about that," said Shawnee. "I don't want to fight with your people."

"You're one of us now," she said. "We're your people too now. But I don't know how you could want to be one of the Real People. They've all gone crazy. Fighting among ourselves. Killing. Claiming rights that don't belong to them. If I see that All Bones, I'll have a thing or two to say to him. You'll see."

"All I want is to be with you," said Shawnee. "But I wish you wouldn't say anything to All Bones about this. We didn't have any real trouble between us. Let's let it go at that."

The Spoiler worked away in silence for a few moments. Then she sat back and looked at her husband.

"You're right," she said. "We should try to avoid trouble with anyone. Do you know what I wanted this bear-skin for? It surprised me. I thought I was too old. But we made a little one, you and I." She patted herself on the stomach with her bloody right hand. "I waited until I was sure of it to tell you. Now I know. It's growing in here right now. I wanted this skin to make it a soft place to sleep."

Shawnee's face registered a little surprise, and then he smiled. He didn't move. He remained sitting against the wall of the house, but he looked at the Spoiler with pride in his eyes.

"This news makes me very happy," he said.

The Spoiler went back to her work with the hint of a smile on her face. Again she worked in silence for a few moments. Then she spoke again.

"Did you see Edohi anywhere along your way today?" she asked.

"No," said Shawnee. "He is probably up on his mountain. He spends much of his time up there, just as he did before the fight with the priests."

"I wanted him to marry Sohi, but the way he is, I'm afraid that he'll never do anything worthwhile again."

"Edohi spends his time thinking about the past, I think," said Shawnee. "He thinks about—his first wife. The war against the priests took his mind away from those thoughts for a brief time, but now the priests are dead, and now his mind has gone back to the old thoughts. He's very sad, and I'm sad for him."

"Well," said the Spoiler, "if he can't bring himself to his senses soon, I'll have to find a way to stop Sohi from thinking about him. She'll have to find herself another man, one that will be useful to her, one that will think about her instead of—the dead."

"Where is Sohi?" asked Shawnee.

"I think she's down at the river's edge," said the Spoiler, "brooding over Edohi. She's as bad as he is. What a pair they would make. Ha."

"Get out of there," shouted Moleskin, and she raised her digging stick up over her head as she rushed toward the other woman. Corn Sifter backed away, startled by the sudden attack.

"What are you doing?" she demanded. "What do you mean by this?"

"You stay out of my garden," said Moleskin. "You were trying to steal my beans. If I hadn't caught you, you would have taken them all. You're a thief."

"What do you mean, your garden?" said Corn Sifter. "I've always worked this plot. My mother worked it before me. You can't chase me out of my own garden plot. I planted those beans, and I've taken care of them all this time."

Corn Sifter took a couple of steps toward Moleskin, but Moleskin raised the long pole up over her shoulder, ready to wield it like a club.

"Come closer to me," she said, "and I'll knock you down. I'll crack your skull with this."

Corn Sifter turned angrily and started to stalk away, but she looked back over her shoulder and spoke one more time.

"You won't get away with this," she said. "Badger droppings."

"That's what you eat," yelled Moleskin.

Corn Sifter kept walking. She went to the entrance to the town, and then she went outside the walls. She hurried on, deliberately, until she came to the small hovel where the old conjurer lived.

"Gone-in-the-Water," she shouted, "are you at home?"

The old man peeked out his doorway.

" '*Siyo*,*'* he said. "What can I do for you?"

"I need your help," said the woman.

Gone-in-the-Water gestured toward a log bench there beside the house.

"Sit down," he said, and he sat down slowly on a large, flat rock nearby, so that he was facing her. He pulled his pipe and tobacco out of a pouch which was hanging at his side. He filled the pipe, then stood up again. He went back inside the house and plucked a live coal out of a clay pot, and he dropped it into the pipe bowl to light the tobacco. Then he went back to the rock outside.

"Now," he said. "What's troubling you?"

"It's Moleskin," said Corn Sifter. "You know that woman?"

Gone-in-the-Water slowly nodded his old hoary head. It was enveloped in blue-gray smoke. Corn Sifter continued.

"She threatened to kill me today," she said. "I was minding my own business, working in my garden, when she came at me with a pole, a long one, the one she uses to poke holes in the ground for the corn. She claimed that I was stealing her beans, that I was in her garden, and she said that she would crack my skull with her pole. I want you to fix something for me. I want her to die."

"I don't use my skills that way," said Gone-in-the-Water. "You should know that about me."

"She could get sick then," said Corn Sifter. "She could

get sick so that she couldn't get up to threaten me again. You could do that much."

"No," said the old man. "When you send evil toward someone, it will come back on you. Sooner or later, it will come back. I don't do those things."

"You don't know how?"

"I know how," he said, "but I won't do it. If you want my help, I can give you something to protect you from harm. That's all I can do."

"Then I'll just go to someone else," said the woman. "There are others."

"Yes, there are others. There are even those who will do what you ask, but I warned you. It will come back at you—sooner or later. My advice is to just take what I can give you for protection and go home."

Corn Sifter stood up stiffly. She glared at the old man, looking at his chest, not at his eyes.

"I know what I want," she said. "I'll find someone else."

Then she turned and stalked away.

Edohi had not visited Kituwah since before the battle at Men's Town, but he remembered the boy, Gnat, and he knew that Gnat was the nephew of Dancing Rabbit, the former Like-a-Pumpkin. He also knew that Gnat's father, Rock Thrower, was a member of his own clan, the Bird People, and he knew that he would be welcome in their home. Walking into Kituwah, he even remembered how to find the house.

On his way through the streets of Kituwah, it seemed to Edohi that everyone recognized him. They knew him as the leader of the revolution against the *Ani-Kutani*, and some of them greeted him like an old friend, some like a hero and others like an outcast to be shunned. He wondered briefly how the family he sought would greet him, and then he was there at their house. The first person he saw was Rock Thrower, and Rock Thrower welcomed him as a kinsman.

In another moment, Walnut, the wife of Rock Thrower, came out of the house. She, too, remembered Edohi, and she offered him food. They ate, and then it was time to talk.

"We haven't seen you for a long time," said Walnut.

"Not since the big fight," said Rock Thrower. "How are things at Ijodi?"

"The same as they are everywhere else," said Edohi. "It seems as if everyone has gone crazy." He looked at Walnut. "I came here to see your brother," he said.

"Dancing Rabbit?" said Walnut.

"Yes," said Edohi. "He who used to be called Like-a-Pumpkin."

Walnut suddenly seemed nervous. She shot a glance toward her husband, but he was looking at the ground. Then Edohi realized what thought had probably gone through their minds. Perhaps they were afraid that Edohi, because of the present unruly situation, was having second thoughts about having allowed the last priest to live. Perhaps they were afraid that he had come to kill Dancing Rabbit.

"I want to talk to him," he said. "I need some advice that no one else can give."

Rock Thrower and Walnut seemed to relax a little, and Rock Thrower reached for his tobacco.

"My brother should be back soon," said Walnut. "He

and my son usually go out into the woods for a time in the day. It's about time for them to return."

"I remember your son," said Edohi. "He's called Gnat. Is that right?"

"Yes," said Walnut.

"He's a good boy. Is he well?"

"Yes. He's very happy, too, to have his uncle back with us. Dancing Rabbit has always been his favorite uncle."

"Your brother is a good one to guide the boy, I think," said Edohi.

"Yes," said Walnut. "I think so."

There was a period of silence then, for the topic on all their minds was the past of Dancing Rabbit, and they all knew that his life as a priest was a controversial and potentially dangerous subject. Then Rock Thrower broke the ominous silence.

"Here they come," he said.

Four

DANCING RABBIT became noticeably nervous when he saw the visitor. Edohi had spared his life, true enough, but he was also the man who had led the slaughter of the priests. He might be having second thoughts, or he might be watching to determine whether or not his decision had been wise. In the mind of Dancing Rabbit, Edohi was a man to be wary of, to be very careful around. Gnat sensed his uncle's apprehension, and he, too, took on a guarded manner.

Edohi spoke to both Dancing Rabbit and Gnat, and his manner was friendly enough. Nothing about him seemed threatening, yet there was that connection, there was that possible danger.

"I really came to see you," Edohi said to Dancing Rabbit. "I want to talk with you about something of great importance, something that concerns all of the Real People. Will you walk with me to some place we can talk in private?"

Dancing Rabbit did not want to walk out to a private place with Edohi, but he couldn't think of a reason to refuse, at least not a reason that he could voice. He gave a short nod.

"Of course," he said. "Come with me."

They took their leave of the others and walked out of the village, Edohi following the lead of Dancing Rabbit. They didn't go far. Dancing Rabbit did not want to take Edohi or anyone else to the secret places where he worked with Gnat on the writing. They went a little ways outside the walls, and then they stopped. Dancing Rabbit turned toward Edohi and waited.

"The Real People are in grave danger," said Edohi. "I guess you know that."

"No," said Dancing Rabbit. "I know of no imminent danger. Is someone going to attack us?"

"It's not that kind of danger," said Edohi. "We killed all the priests. Well, almost all. Now we have no authority, none that anyone recognizes. We are fighting among ourselves over things that should not matter, or things that should be easily resolved. If something doesn't happen to change things soon, we'll be like packs of wild dogs, or even worse."

"Yes," said Dancing Rabbit. "I have observed that behavior, but why have you come to me? There's nothing I can do."

Edohi paced away from Dancing Rabbit and stood for a moment in thought.

"Dancing Rabbit," he said, "do you know why we killed the priests?"

"I wasn't here," said Dancing Rabbit, "and since my return, I haven't spoken to anyone about it. I've always thought it best, for my own safety, to stay away from that subject."

Somehow Edohi had not before that very moment considered the fears that might be lurking in the breast of Dancing Rabbit.

"Of course," he said. "I think I understand. Well, let me try to explain it to you."

Edohi talked about the abuses of the *Ani-Kutani*, and even though it pained him to recall, he told Dancing Rabbit what had happened to his wife. He spoke of the discussions and the meeting which had preceded the attack on Men's Town, and the difficulty of making that final decision.

"We killed the priests for taking too much power to themselves and for misusing that power," he said. "We attacked the men, not our beliefs. We believe the way we have always believed. But now we have no guidance."

"Why have you come to me, Edohi?" asked Dancing Rabbit.

"Because you are the only one left. You were a *Kutani*. You know the rituals and the ceremonies. You can bring them back."

"No," said Dancing Rabbit. "I cannot. Surely, if I try to lead the ceremonies, someone will kill me. I lead a quiet life. I don't want to become prominent. I especially don't want to become prominent in the role of a priest."

"Then what can be done?"

"I don't know. I only know that I am not the one to do it."

"Will you think about the problem?" asked Edohi. "Will you talk with me further about it, in private, as we have been talking here?"

Dancing Rabbit wrinkled his brow in agitated thought. He considered the danger to himself, and he considered the danger to the Real People. Edohi was right, of course. He knew that. He had seen the spreading chaos, and he himself had worried about the future.

"Come again in four days," he said. "We'll talk some more."

Moleskin had a sudden painful cramp in her stomach. The pain was so sharp and so intense that she cried out. She clutched at her middle with both hands and doubled over, nearly falling to her knees there in front of her house. Tears came to her eyes, and her face twisted into a grotesque mask of agony. Just across the road at her own house, the Spoiler heard the cry, looked and saw Moleskin doubled over. She ran to her and put an arm around her.

"Moleskin," she said. "What is it? What's wrong with you?"

"My stomach," said Moleskin, speaking through clenched teeth and between gasps, "is hurting me. The pain is terrible."

"Can you walk?"

"Ah. I don't know."

"It's not far to the house of Gone-in-the-Water," said the Spoiler. "Come on. I'll help you."

Moleskin still twisted in agony, even with the Spoiler's support. She could barely stand, much less walk. The Spoiler looked over toward her own house.

"Sohi," she called. "Come here. We need your help."

Sohi came running, and the two healthy women, one on either side, supported Moleskin, and though she groaned and cried out, they did manage to get her to the house of Gone-in-the-Water. The old man heard them coming, and he stepped outside to meet them. He gave Moleskin only a brief look.

"Take her inside," he said.

She stayed there all night, the old man mixing medicine, smoking, now and then giving Moleskin tobacco to smoke, mumbling unintelligible words in a low, quiet voice. And in the morning she was better. She was tired and weak, but she was no longer in pain. He handed her a small bundle, and she took it in both her hands and held it close to her bosom.

"Use it just the way I told you," he said. "Everything will be all right. Someone is sending this thing to you, and this that I have given you will turn it away and send it back. Give it seven days. If you have any more pain after that, come and see me again. But I don't believe that you will have any more trouble."

"*Wado*, Gone-in-the-Water," said Moleskin. "Without your help, I think I would have died."

"Go home now," said the old man, "and rest."

He stood in his doorway and watched as she walked away, and he thought about the visit Corn Sifter had paid him earlier. Corn Sifter had gone to some other conjurer, someone with no sense of professional ethics, and that person, whoever it might be, along with Corn Sifter was responsible for the trouble Moleskin was having.

Gone-in-the-Water's face was puckered in troubled thought. He had sent Corn Sifter away because he would not do harm to a person with his powers and his knowledge. But now someone had come to him for relief from pain, and he had helped her. That was what he was supposed to do. Except if another was causing the pain by the use of another conjurer, Gone-in-the-Water's protection would harm someone. It would harm the sender of the evil medicine by turning it back to its source. It was a dilemma which the old man had never found a way around. He had no choice. If he helped the victim, he would harm the instigator.

It was something that always bothered the old conjurer when he had a situation like this one, but there was no solution. He had decided long ago that it was a thing that he would just have to live with. It was a thing that he would undoubtedly die with as well. It was like weak eyes, a sore back, painful joints or withered, wrinkled skin. It was just a part of his life. He didn't like it, but it was there, and it would be until the end.

"Uncle," said Gnat, "is everything all right?"

"I don't know," said Dancing Rabbit.

"What did Edohi want with you?"

"He said that he wanted my advice."

"Advice about what?"

Dancing Rabbit looked at his nephew for a brief moment. He put a hand on the young man's head.

"Yes," he said. "I can tell you. You're young, yet I've already given you a man's burden. He said he wanted me to play the role of priest, to lead the ceremonies again. He said that the people need them to give some order to their lives again."

"I don't understand," said Gnat.

"You've seen how the people are acting since—the killing of the priests," said Dancing Rabbit.

"You mean the crazy way people have become? Always fussing and fighting with each other?"

"Yes."

"And Edohi thinks the ceremonies could stop all that?"

"Yes."

"Will you do it, Uncle?"

"No," said Dancing Rabbit. "I told him I would not."

"But why?"

"They killed all the priests except me," said Dancing Rabbit. "Every day I think that maybe someone will decide that they made a mistake by letting me live. If I lead the old ceremonies, it will only remind everyone of my previous life as Like-a-Pumpkin, the *Kutani*. It would be a foolish thing for me to do, I think."

"I see," said Gnat. "I think that you're right. I think that you should not lead the ceremonies."

"But, Nephew," said Dancing Rabbit, "what if Edohi is right? What if the people need the ceremonies to give order to their lives once again? What if I am the only person left who can save the people from themselves? What if, in trying to save myself, I allow the people to be destroyed?"

"Is that possible?" said Gnat.

"I'm afraid that it might be possible," said Dancing Rabbit, "and that is why I told Edohi to come back in four days to talk with me again. I have to think about it, and I have to seek some guidance from somewhere."

Gnat stared at the ground, wondering what to say. He didn't want his uncle's life endangered, but he was horrified at the thought that the Real People could cease to exist. It was a dilemma such as he had never before faced in his short life, and he wished that it would just go away, that it would somehow resolve itself.

"Nephew," said Dancing Rabbit.

"Yes?"

"If anything should happen to me, you will carry our secret alone. We have to work harder to make sure that you remember the symbols perfectly, that they are set in your mind so that you will never forget them. Do you understand?"

"Yes," said Gnat. "I understand."

Pot Kicker was as quiet as he could be. He was hidden in thick brush and the unsuspecting deer moved closer. He waited until his shot was sure, and he drew back the string and almost silently uttered the words which would help his arrow on its way to the mark. Then he released it. There was a twang and a swish and a thud, and the deer gave a short leap forward, then fell. Pot Kicker ran to its side. He dropped to his knees there beside it and pulled out his knife, but before he could slice the throat, Beavertail stepped out of the woods to confront him, a ball-headed warclub in his hand.

"What are you doing here?" said Beavertail. "This is the territory of the Bird People. You have no right to be here, and you have no right to that deer."

"It's my deer," said Pot Kicker. "I just killed it."

"But you had no right to kill it, not here in this territory. You're not a Bird Person."

"No," said Pot Kicker. "I am of the Paint People, but I can hunt where I choose. The Paint People have always had that privilege."

"Move away from that deer," said Beavertail.

Pot Kicker stood up, his knife in his hand.

"You'll have to try to move me," he said. "I know my rights."

"And I know mine," said Beavertail. He raised his war-club high over his head and rushed at Pot Kicker. Pot Kicker stepped aside and dodged the swinging warclub. At the same time, he took a swipe at Beavertail with his knife, and the tip of the blade left a thin red line across the side of Beavertail. Beavertail whirled in anger to face Pot Kicker again. Pot Kicker jabbed at him with the knife, and Beavertail brought the heavy club down across Pot Kicker's forearm with a loud crack. Pot Kicker screamed in pain and dropped his knife. The bone in his arm was broken. Then Beavertail swung the club again, smashing it into the side of Pot Kicker's head. Pot Kicker dropped to the ground, a lifeless lump.

Five

SEVERAL MEMBERS of the Paint Clan had gathered at the home of the sister of Pot Kicker. They had already conducted his funeral rites, and they were still in mourning, but this was a business meeting, and the business at hand was business of the clan. There was no mystery about the killing of Pot Kicker. Beavertail had openly boasted of the deed. And that was the business of the meeting.

"My brother's death must be avenged," said Willow.

"Yes," said Burntwood. "Things are out of balance. The Bird People have taken one of our lives. We must have the life of a Bird Person to make things right again."

The mother of Willow, and, of course, of the dead Pot Kicker, was sitting in a corner of the house. She was old, small and withered, but when she spoke up the others all grew silent and listened.

"There's been enough talk," she said. "The decision has been made. Now who will do the deed?"

"I will," said Burntwood.

"Then go," said the old woman, "and do it. Before more time is wasted. The spirit that is out there wandering needs to be put to rest."

And so the meeting was ended.

Rock Thrower had all the fish he needed for the day. It had been a good day, and he was well satisfied. He gathered up his nets along with his catch and started for home. He was not far from Kituwah. The narrow path from the river's edge through the woods would get him home in a short while. Yes, he thought, it had been a good day. He had done everything just right. Everyone knew that the spirits of killed animals might seek revenge for the death, so Rock Thrower had caught his first fish and then whispered to the side of its head, "It was not I who caught you. It was a Catawba person." Then he had thrown the fish back in. If any fish spirit should seek vengeance for this catch of Rock Thrower's, it would seek out some unsuspecting Catawba. Rock Thrower felt good and safe and a little smug.

He was anxious to show this fine catch of fish to his wife and his son, and even to his brother-in-law, Dancing Rabbit. Dancing Rabbit, Rock Thrower thought, was a fine fellow. If one had to have a brother-in-law living in his wife's house with them, he couldn't have had a better, he thought. He could think of much worse. Dancing Rabbit was modest and humble. He tried to stay out of the way, and he tried to help out in every way he could. He also took his responsibility as Gnat's maternal uncle very seriously, and he spent much time with the boy.

Well, Rock Thrower thought, they would all eat well

this day on these fine fish. Then he was startled by the sudden, unexpected, shrill human imitation of the cry of the wild turkey. It was an unmistakable sound, and its meaning was always clear. It was the war cry of the Real People. It meant that somebody was about to strike, about to kill, and it came from behind him. He dropped his burden to the ground and turned to face the challenge just in time to see Burntwood emerge from the woods, to see the bow drawn and then released, to see the beginning of the flight of the arrow. Then it thudded into his chest, and there was no real pain, just an instant of shock, and then there was nothing.

When Edohi returned to Kituwah to visit again with Dancing Rabbit, he found the family there in mourning for the death of Rock Thrower. The dead man had been the husband of Walnut, the father of Gnat and the brother-in-law of Dancing Rabbit. Therefore they mourned. But he had also been a clan relative of Edohi, and so Edohi, too, was obliged to mourn his loss. Mourning, though, was not enough for Walnut. She was yet too angry to be sad, and she thirsted for justice for the loss of her husband, but such justice was the business of the clans.

"You are a war leader," she said to Edohi. "And he was your clan brother. You should be the one to avenge his death. Is that why you came here today? To avenge his death for the Bird People?"

"I didn't know about the death," said Edohi, "until I arrived here today. I'm sorry to hear it. I came here today to keep my meeting with your brother on another matter." He gave Dancing Rabbit a quick glance. "Perhaps we should postpone our meeting, as urgent as it is. This is probably not a good time."

"This is the best time for you to deal with your clan affairs," said Walnut. "One of your people has been killed by the Paint People. What are you going to do? Just go home? You have to do something. It's your duty."

"Sister," said Dancing Rabbit, "don't be angry with Edohi. Try to be patient. I'll talk with him."

He motioned for Edohi to follow, and he left the house and walked toward the edge of the village. Outside of town, he stopped and turned to face Edohi.

"Edohi," he said, "I know why you came to see me, of course, but this other business must be dealt with first. It's part of the other, larger issue, and I don't believe anyone will listen to you until it's been settled."

"Yes," said Edohi. "I know. But I want to stop this senseless killing, this endless cycle of vengeance. I don't want to take part in it."

"We all know," said Dancing Rabbit, "that things must always be balanced between the clans, as with all other things on this earth. Otherwise, so we've been taught, our world may end."

"Yes, I know, but—"

"Someone from your clan will take care of this matter. One way or another. If not you, then someone else."

"Yes."

"Don't you think it would be better if you took the responsibility upon yourself?"

"But I just told you," said Edohi, a little exasperated, "that I don't want to take part in these clan killings, these revenge killings. Once they get started, there's no end to them."

"That's why you must find a way to bring them to an end. Edohi, my friend," said Dancing Rabbit, "there is more than one way to restore the balance. But one way or the other, it must be done if we are going to go ahead with our plans."

Edohi looked at Dancing Rabbit, just for a moment. Dancing Rabbit had not before said that he would help. He had only agreed to talk further with Edohi.

"Then you will help me?" he said.

"Yes. I've lost a brother-in-law," said Dancing Rabbit. "You were right. This chaos must come to an end. Somehow you and I must find a way to restore some order in this land."

"All right," said Edohi. "Tell your sister that I will take care of this problem. I'll go and find the other Bird People in Kituwah, and I'll go to the Paint People."

And Edohi's reputation was such that the Bird People immediately agreed to allow him to set things right between them and the Paint People, although they neglected to ask him just how he would accomplish that feat. And Edohi told them that it would be done within seven days, one way or the other.

Gone-in-the-Water groaned and rubbed his eyes with the backs of his wrinkled old hands. He had been napping. He yawned, and, with some effort, he sat up on his bench-like cot. He reached up with both hands to brush his long hair back out of his face, and he found it matted and tangled in knots.

"Ah," he said as he pulled out a fistful of hair. "Where are you? What have you done to me? Tied my hair in knots while I slept? Just wait until I find you, you two worthless little scamps. Where are you? Noisy? Ugly? Where are you hiding?"

He stood up and stretched, and his old bones popped and cracked. Then he looked carefully around the room, taking more time to study the corners. He looked behind a large clay pot which stood against the wall by poking at it and tilting it with his walking stick, but he found nothing there.

"So," he said, "tied knots in my hair and then ran away. Ah, well, I don't care. I have more important things to worry about."

He continued as if talking to himself, but he raised his voice just a little as he kept poking about the small house.

"I have bigger things to do," he said. "Important things. I don't need to be bothered with little people just now anyway. It's a good thing they're gone. Yes. A very good thing."

He turned his back to the door and started to pick over the strange assortment of items which lay in disarray on a small shelf on the back wall. He stood still for a moment and listened, then slowly he turned his head to peer over his shoulder at the doorway.

"Aha," he said. "So there you are. I thought so. So you've come back, you two. You couldn't stand to think that I would do something important without having you around to poke your noses in it, could you? What? What is it that I'm going to do? You'd like to know, wouldn't you? Well, you'll find out soon enough. As long as you're here, you might as well make yourselves useful. Come over here, Noisy. I'll tell you what to do. What? Be patient, Ugly. I'll get to you soon enough. We have lots of things to do to get ready for this thing."

. . . .

Groundhog's Brother saw Edohi coming toward him. He was standing there on the edge of the Kituwah town square talking with other members of the Paint Clan who lived in Kituwah. Like almost everyone else, Groundhog's Brother knew Edohi because of his role in the recent uprising against the priests, and he knew that Edohi was a Bird Person. He braced himself for a possible conflict, for he also knew that the Bird People would be seeking revenge for the death of Rock Thrower. He stood watching and waiting as Edohi came closer, and he waited for Edohi to speak first.

" *'Siyo,*" said Edohi. "I'm looking for Paint People."

"You've found us," said Groundhog's Brother. "We're all Paints. What do you want with us?"

"I'm Edohi of the Bird People, from Ijodi."

"We know you. Everyone knows Edohi. I'm called Groundhog's Brother. So what do you want of us? A life? Did you come because of Rock Thrower? If so, I'm ready to fight you here."

"I didn't come to fight," said Edohi. "There's been too much fighting and too much killing among the Real People. We no longer need any enemies. We are killing each other."

"Then what?" said Groundhog's Brother. He looked at Edohi suspiciously, and his kinsmen gathered close around.

"It's true," said Edohi, "that there are some among my people, the Bird People, who want a life from you in exchange for the life of Rock Thrower. It's the old way. And we all know that it's necessary to maintain balance on this earth."

"But you did not come to fight?" said Groundhog's Brother.

"No," said Edohi. "Nor to kill. The Bird People have lost a man because of you. Give us another to take his place. Then there will be no need for another killing. Then the killing can stop here."

"Who should we give you?" said Groundhog's Brother. "We have no prisoners, no one to give. Besides, we think that everything is already balanced. Rock Thrower was killed to pay for Pot Kicker. The Bird People have paid the price for their own actions. Go home and leave us alone."

"I could do that," said Edohi, "but someone else would seek revenge. Not all my kinsmen think as I do. I'm trying to stop the killing. Suppose I could provide you with someone to give away?"

"What do you mean?"

"If I could bring you an outsider and give him to you, would you then give him to the Bird People to replace the one who has been killed?"

"Would the rest of your clan accept that payment?" said Groundhog's Brother.

"I don't know," said Edohi, "but I will try to convince them that would be the best way. If I succeed, will you go along with me on this exchange?"

Groundhog's Brother turned around and gathered his clan brothers in close. Edohi turned and walked away a few steps to allow them a brief, private conversation. In a moment, Groundhog's Brother stepped out again from the gathering and faced Edohi.

"Come back to talk with us again tomorrow," he said. "We'll have an answer for you then."

"I'll be here tomorrow," said Edohi, and he turned to walk away.

Before leaving Kituwah, he stopped to talk with the Bird People there, and they agreed to wait for him before planning any action against the Paint Clan. He took his leave and started home. He had to talk to some people there, too, or his plan would never work. He had to talk to his mother, and he had to talk to the Spoiler. But he would have to talk to her through a second party. Even though his wife was dead, the Spoiler was still his mother-in-law, and he could not speak directly to her.

Six

IT WAS A BRIGHT, clear night. *Ani-chuja*, the six boys, were there, and so was the Arm. And *Gili-utsuh-stanuhyi*, Where-the-Dog-Ran, was plain in the sky. Gone-in-the-Water had been sound asleep for several hours, but his eyes popped open at once, as if someone had made a noise to wake him. He sat up, awake and alert, and in a moment, he stood. He had been sleeping naked, but he was still nearly so even after he had dressed, for he wore only breechclout and moccasins.

"Wake up, you two," he said in a loud, clear voice. "Noisy. Ugly. It's time to go. Wake up, you lazy little people."

He picked up a pouch which he had prepared earlier. It contained tobacco and his pipe, and he found the clay pot in which he always kept glowing embers. Then he grasped his long walking staff and with all his paraphernalia headed for the door.

"I'm leaving," he said. "Come along if you're interested. If not, go ahead and sleep away your worthless lives. You'll still be asleep when the world comes to an end."

He paused in the doorway and glanced back into the room.

"Oh," he said. "So you've decided to come along after all, have you? Well, come on then. Do as you like. I don't care one way or the other."

He walked a few feet away from his house to a place where a narrow path went into the woods, and he turned onto that path.

"What?" he said. "What's that? Have you forgotten already? I told you where we're going and what we're going to do. Oh, all right. We're going to the river, and we're going to prop up the world. That's what. Now keep quiet and just follow me along."

He walked farther, deeper into the woods, and for a while the only noises were the ordinary sounds of the night and the soft padding of the footsteps on the path. Then he stopped abruptly and turned around, looking down onto the path behind him.

"What's that?" he said. "Of course you've never seen it before. It's reserved for very special times. It's not to be used lightly. Only when the fate of all the Real People is concerned, when our whole world is in imminent danger, that's when one goes to the water for the whole people all at once, that's the time when we must work to prop up the world. Now keep quiet and follow me along."

He turned again and resumed his walk along the narrow path. The light from the moon and stars was shut out from the path by the thick canopy of leafy branches above, but Gone-in-the-Water knew his way. He could have walked this particular path with his eyes closed. In a short time, he came out of the woods to a wide bank alongside the river. There it was not so dark, and there he placed his pouch and his pot of coals on the ground beside the water, and he sat on the trunk of a nearby fallen tree to rest. It took a little longer for him to catch his breath than he had thought it would, but at last he was ready to proceed. He stood up, leaving his staff leaning there against the fallen tree.

"Ah," he said, slowly straightening himself up, "I'm getting old."

He walked to the pouch where he had left it on the ground, and he bent over with a groan to pick it up.

"Now you two stay out of my way," he said. "Just sit over there and watch everything I do. This is probably the only chance you'll ever have to see this. Pay attention."

He opened up the pouch and took out the pipe. Then he poured the tobacco out on the ground in a neat, peaked pile and straightened himself again to look up at the stars.

"It's time to go to work now," he said, and he turned to face east. He stood for a moment in silence and took a deep breath.

"Hey, you, up there in the Seventh Heaven," he said. "I've just come here into your light, in there with the seven clans. All my enemies are confused. They're stumbling around in the dark.

"But I am standing upright in the light and walking straight ahead. I am walking along on the White Path just where you put me. You, Ancient Red One, you have put me there.

"And you, Ancient White One, you will be right beside

me there on the path. Everywhere I go on this earth, you will be there with me. I am dressed in beautiful clothes, standing there in the light. The seven clans will all stand in awe of me. The brightness of the light there on the White Path where I am walking will make them squint their eyes. The smoke of my Ancient Tobacco will cover my enemies.

"And you Red Uk'ten', you rose up from the deep waters to move inside my body. You said so. And I will have the jaws and the teeth of the Red Mountain Lion, and each of the seven clans will make room for me in their midst and will give me a place to sit and a place to eat."

Gone-in-the-Water paused to catch his breath. He sucked in the cool night air deeply until his lungs were filled. Then he continued with his recitation.

"Red Thunder will be in me, and the Red Raven will move in my body. I am everywhere on earth, and everything is in me. My name is Gone-in-the-Water and I am a Wolf Man. I have come here to shield myself with the Red Uk'ten'.

"My clan is the Wolf Clan, and I've come here for a shield from the Red Thunder. My enemies wander about aimlessly in the dark, but you, Ancient White One, you have just placed me on the White Path in the bright light of the Sunland."

Gone-in-the-Water said the words all over again six more times until he had said them once for each of the seven clans. Then he squatted beside the tobacco, filled his pipe bowl and lit it with an ember from the clay pot. Smoking, he stood again, still facing east, and he blew his smoke in that direction. Then he began walking in a circle. He stopped after a quarter of the way around and blew smoke toward the north. He did the same thing at the west and at the south, and he finished back where he had begun, again facing the east.

By then the tobacco in his pipe was used up, and he squatted again and refilled the bowl and relit the pipe. He made the same circle with the same stops seven times, once for each of the seven clans. Then he sat down to rest. It was going to be a long night. For the ceremony to be effective, it had to be repeated, from beginning to end, six more times. If he timed it just right, and he must, he would finish the seventh and final performance just as the sun was peeking out from under the eastern edge of the Sky Vault in the morning.

"Hm? No," he said. "It's not over yet. It has to be done some more. If you can't take it, go on home. I don't need you two."

And he did it a second time, almost exactly as before. Perhaps he spoke and moved a bit more slowly, but that was the only difference. He paused again to rest.

"What did you say, Noisy? You don't think I'll last the night, eh? Ha. You'll see. You and your little friend will probably be lying there on the ground and snoring while I'm still at work here. Ha. Now I've rested enough."

He went through the third repetition of the ceremony, and he could feel his old bones beginning to ache, but he was not sleepy. And so he rested again, and he went through the ceremony again. Three times to go. He looked up at the stars, and he looked at the tobacco there on the ground. The timing seemed to be right, and it looked as if there would be plenty of tobacco. He got up to go again, the fifth time. And he knew that he was slower than before, and his brittle old body was feeling very stiff.

Yet he made it through with no mistakes. Five rounds done. Two to go. He was wide awake. His bones were hurting more and more, and he was so stiff he could hardly bend his joints. This time he rested longer than before.

"No, no," he said. "I'm all right. Just a little sore. I'll make it through all right."

But when he got up to begin the sixth round, he took his staff with him, and he leaned on it heavily while he worked. And when he was done, he made his way slowly and painfully back to the fallen tree to rest.

"You two surprise me," he said. "I thought you'd be asleep by now. You probably thought that I'd be dead, but I'm still going. I'll keep going until I'm done, until the sun comes out again. You think you can keep up with me? Can you stay awake? Can you? Ha. You'll see who's too old, you two."

He got up to do it again. The seventh time. And he staggered and almost tripped and fell. He groaned out loud as he dropped back to the ground beside the fallen tree. He leaned back against the tree trunk and sighed a heavy sigh. He was breathing heavily.

"One more time," he said. "Ah. I don't know. I don't know if I can make it. I don't think I can even stand up from here again. What? No. You don't know. My bones are aching. I'm tired. I'm more than tired. I'm worn out. I might just lie right here and die. I can't get up another time. What? No. Not even with the staff. My strength is gone. I thought I could do it, but I'm just too old. Too old."

Then he was quiet. His breathing became steady, long, deep, slow breaths, his bony chest heaving with each inhalation. The old skin looked dry and brittle and thin there in the light of the stars and the moon. He rested, and the moments passed, slowly, painfully and anxiously.

"Eh? What?" he said, lifting his head a little. "What's that? I know the time is almost up. You don't have to tell me. The sun will look out soon. I know. But there's nothing I can do. I'm used up. My time is past. What are you doing? Noisy? Ugly? Stop pushing me. I can't do it. Stop. I— Ah."

He was on his feet, and his staff was in his hand. He stood for a moment, weaving unsteadily on his tired, old feet. Then he began shuffling along, barely moving, back toward the tobacco once again. The seventh round. The final round. This would be the last time, if he could only make it all the way through. It occurred to him that he probably shouldn't have boasted so to the little people there. Perhaps he had brought this on himself with his bragging.

"If I can last through it," he said. "If— All right. All right, you two. Step back out of the way now. I'll do it."

And he did. His voice was weak, but he said the words. He said them right, and he said them the proper number of times. His walk was unsteady, but he kept his feet. And he walked the prescribed circle the right direction and the right number of times. And when he squatted down to get the tobacco, he was somehow able to stand up again. Each time. And then he was done, and then the sun emerged from under the eastern edge of the Sky Vault to redden the horizon over there. Then, one painful step at a time, his feet scraping the ground, never lifting up, Gone-in-the-Water walked back to his resting spot.

Carefully, as if he thought that he might break himself, he got down on the ground and stretched himself out to sleep. He knew better than to try to make it home.

"Noisy," he said, panting, gasping for breath, his words coming out in halting, strange patterns. "Ugly. I'd never have made it without your help. *Wado.* Thank you, my little friends. But now I have to sleep. I'll go home later. When I've slept. What? You'll stay here with me? Thank you. Thank you."

And he drifted off to sleep, a deep and restful sleep.

Seven

MOLESKIN was feeling much better, although she was still a bit weak. But the pain was gone, and she was grateful to Gone-in-the-Water for that relief. She was harboring a great deal of resentment toward Corn Sifter for what had happened to her, for she was certain in her mind that Corn Sifter was responsible for the attack. Corn Sifter had found herself some conjurer with no ethical compunction, someone who would do anything to anyone for his pay. Or for her pay. It could be man or woman. Moleskin wondered where Corn Sifter had gone. She wondered just who had sent the sickness to her.

Whoever it was, she thought, Gone-in-the-Water must have more power, for he had turned the sickness away from her. Gone-in-the-Water was a good man with a strong sense of ethics, and that was probably the reason that his power was so great.

Anyway, Moleskin was feeling better. She thought that

she would probably feel well enough in another day or so
to go back to work in her field. She wondered if she would
have another encounter with Corn Sifter there when that
time came.

Edohi had spent the night in the *osi*, the hothouse or
winter house beside his mother's larger house. Since the
death of his wife he had no home of his own to go to, so
he had gone back to his mother. He hadn't really spent
much time there. He stayed out on the mountain or away
in the woods much of the time. And when he did stay at
his mother's house, he felt as if he was somehow intrud-
ing. It no longer seemed to him like his home. He stayed
out in the *osi*.

In the morning, he waited until he heard his parents
stirring outside, and then he crawled out of his shelter.

" '*Siyo*, Edohi," said Big Bear. "We're going down to
the river. Do you want to come along?"

"Of course," said Edohi. "It's the proper way to start
the day."

"Yes," said Wild Hemp, "but not many bother to do it
anymore. The people are not acting properly these days.
Not since—"

"Not since we killed the priests," said Edohi. "Come
on. Let's go to the water."

They walked together to the river's edge, and then they
waded in together until the water was up to their waists.
Then they bent their knees and went down farther, and
they ducked their heads under the fresh running water.
Edohi came back up for air, shaking the water from his
head. It was a good feeling, wading into the river to start a
new day.

"Look," said Wild Hemp, gesturing with her chin downstream. "The Spoiler is there with her family."

Edohi looked and saw the Spoiler, Shawnee, Sohi, Agili and Stinging Ant all in the river.

"The whole village should be in here with us," he said.

"Yes," said Wild Hemp. "They should be. But no one can tell them anything anymore."

"Where is my uncle?" said Edohi.

"He went hunting," said Big Bear.

"He would be in here with us if he were home," said Wild Hemp. "My brother is not like those fools. He still does what's right."

They left the water and sat on the bank to dry in the warm sun. Edohi stretched out on his back and stared at the white puffs of clouds rolling overhead.

"Mother," he said. "There is something I have to do. You know the Paint People have killed one of our people over at Kituwah?"

"Yes," said Wild Hemp. "I heard something about that."

"I talked to some of the Paint People over there, and they said that the killing was justified. They said that one of ours had killed one of theirs first. They said that they killed this one only in retaliation, only to set things right again."

"Is it true?" asked Wild Hemp. "Is that the way it happened?"

"Who knows anymore where it started," said Edohi, "or where it will end? I only know that there are some of ours who want to kill one of them now."

"And you disagree?"

"It's got to stop somewhere, Mother. I saw Gone-in-the-Water, and he said that my job is not over. It didn't end there at Men's Town. He said I still have work to do. As long as our people are acting crazy, I have work to do."

He sat up and stared at the river, and he thought how simple it would be to just put everyone in the water and allow Long Man to wash away the craziness from them all.

"I wish my uncle was here," he said.

"He should be back before too much longer," said Wild Hemp.

"I can't wait for him," Edohi said. "Too many things could happen while I wait."

"So what will you do?" asked his mother.

Edohi turned toward her, suddenly eager.

"I want you to help me, Mother," he said. "I can't do this without your help and without the help of the Spoiler. I can't talk to her, but you can."

"Of course, I'll help," said Wild Hemp. "What is it you want me to do?"

"There's a lot to be done," said Edohi, "but first I want to try to stop all this senseless killing, this killing of Real People by Real People, and how can I talk to others about this problem if my own clan is involved in the killing? So the first thing I must do—we must do—is to stop our own Bird People from retaliating against the Paint Clan."

"How can we do that, Edohi?" said Wild Hemp. "Will they listen to us about that?"

"I don't know, Mother, but the only way they might listen is if we offer them an alternative to the killing. If the Paints would give us a man to adopt into our clan, then the balance would be restored without a killing."

"Will they do that?"

"I don't know."

"I can start talking to them to find out."

"No, Mother," said Edohi. "I can talk to them. I want you to talk with the Spoiler."

Two days' journey away from Ijodi, a band of *Ani-Suwali* warriors were making their way through the woods. They were neighbors of the Real People. They lived to the northeast, and there had been constant though intermittent warfare between the two peoples for as long as anyone could remember. The Suwali People came out of the woods into a clearing by the river, and they were looking down upon a town of the Real People. It was not a border town, and it had no fence for protection.

"It's the town they call Taskigi," said a big Suwali man.

"In a little while," said another, "they'll be calling it 'the place where Taskigi used to be.' Come on."

The Suwalis set up a howl, raised their weapons and rushed into Taskigi. The inhabitants of the town were taken completely by surprise. Some ran for their weapons. Some ran for the woods. One big warrior of Taskigi flung himself at the Suwalis, wildly swinging a warclub. He cracked two skulls before a Suwali came up behind him and bashed him over the head. The Taskigi warrior fell heavily to the ground, knocked unconscious by the blow. It was Cuts-Off-Their-Heads, the man so renamed because of his grisly assignment just before the attack on Men's Town.

He lay there no longer aware of what was happening in his town. He did not know that all who stayed to fight were killed. He did not see the few escape into the woods. And he was unaware that the Suwalis had set fire to every house in Taskigi. He came to his senses sometime later, and it was dark. His head hurt, and he did not know at first where he was. He discovered that his arms were tightly bound, and as he looked around, he slowly took in the information that he was somewhere away from home at a campsite. A small fire burned.

Slowly his eyes grew used to searching the darkness around him, and he saw that he was surrounded by sleeping Suwalis. So that was it, he thought. He had been captured by the Suwalis. They had not left anyone awake that he could see, and he decided to try to slip away from them. But when he tried to sit up, he discovered that he was tied by a long leash to a tree. He tested the thongs that bound his wrists behind his back, and he found them tight, secure. There was nothing he could do but wait.

Well after the departure of the Suwali raiding party, people began to re-emerge from the woods outside of Taskigi. Slowly they made their way back down to what remained of their town. And there was not much except ashes. Looking at their dead, they wailed. They spent the night in the woods and the next morning dealing with the bodies. When they had done, they were gathered there together, a ragged, wretched lot.

"What shall we do?" said a man.

"Let's go to Ijodi," said a woman. "They'll take us in over there, and there is where Edohi lives. He led the attack on Men's Town. Perhaps he'll lead us against these *Ani-Suwali* to take our revenge."

"Yes," said another woman. "You're right. We'll go to Ijodi for shelter and for help."

Without another word, she turned and started to walk.

The others fell in behind her, and the somber procession began its journey toward Ijodi. They had found nothing of value left in the ashes, and so they traveled with nothing other than the clothes they wore. From Taskigi to Ijodi was but a day's traveling time, but it would be a long way to walk for these people on this unhappy day.

Corn Sifter felt tired. There were some things she wanted to do yet, but she just did not have the energy. She didn't feel sick, just tired, and so it took her a while to realize what was the matter.

"It's that Moleskin," she said. "She's found someone to work his tricks on me. To make me sick. Probably to kill me. This tiredness is just the first sign. If I don't do something soon, I'll get sick and then die. I have to go back to the old woman."

She watched over her shoulder as she left the town, for she did not want to be seen. The old woman to whom she referred was a conjurer who lived outside of Kituwah. She was known far and wide as a woman with no conscience and no ethics, but she was also known as a woman of much power. She was feared and hated and mostly avoided, and her name was Breaks-Things-Up.

Corn Sifter did not want anyone to know that she was consulting with Breaks-Things-Up, and that was the reason for her surreptitious departure from Ijodi. It was also the reason she chose the path through the woods and along the steep mountainsides rather than the open road. But she was tired, and she was not even halfway to her goal when she began to worry that she might not have the strength to make it. Perhaps, she thought with dread, she had waited too long. She had not recognized the weariness for what it was. And the farther she walked, the more tired she became. Each step became more difficult than the last one. She slipped and fell on the trail more than once, and soon both her knees were scraped, and the palms of her hands were bruised from breaking her falls on the rocky trail.

But she had to keep going. She had to make it to the home of Breaks-Things-Up in order to get some protection against whatever it was that was sapping her strength. She was convinced that if she failed to make this trip, she would die.

The path had become so narrow that it was barely perceptible, and it was running along a ridge that dropped off steeply down to a rocky riverbank. She stepped on a loose rock and lost her balance. Her feet shot off over the edge, and she landed hard on her buttocks on the rocky trail. Her feet pointed toward the river below, and she was slipping. She grasped at the rocks on the ledge, but they were all small and loose, and she kept slipping. She twisted, rolling over onto her stomach and grasping with her hands for something, anything to get a grip on, but she kept slipping, and then she fell.

Shawnee was climbing the mountain just outside of Ijodi. He was headed for the place where he had met and talked with Edohi before, the place where he knew that Edohi went to be alone. His wife, the Spoiler, had told him that Edohi wanted to see him about something. She had gotten the message from Edohi's mother. It was something of some importance. More than that she did not know.

So Shawnee was climbing the mountain. He wondered what it could be that Edohi wanted to see him about in this secluded spot. But the Spoiler had asked him to go, and so he was going. He would do anything that she asked him to do. If he knew that she wanted something, even if she did not ask, he would do it.

He reached the top of the mountain and stood for a moment looking around. He saw no sign of Edohi. Likely he had gotten there ahead of time. He walked over to the large rock where Edohi often sat, and he looked out over the road below and the town of Ijodi, his new home. And then he heard a noise behind him, and he turned to see seven men standing there. They were heavily armed and their faces were grim. Three of them held bows with arrows nocked and strings drawn, and the arrows were aimed at his chest. One man, holding a warclub in his right hand down at his side, stepped forward.

"You're the Shawnee?" he asked.

"Yes," said Shawnee. "What do you want with me?"

"I am Groundhog's Brother of the Paint Clan in Kituwah," said the other. "These are all my clan brothers, and you are our prisoner."

Eight

CORN SIFTER had decided that she was going to die. She was cut and bruised all over from her fall, and she was almost certain that her leg was broken. She was not on a heavily traveled road but a rarely used back trail, so she did not expect anyone to just happen by. And she had been weak to begin with. She thought that she had already been dying, and she had been on her way to see Breaks-Things-Up in a desperate attempt to save her life. But she had fallen, and she was hurt, and there was no way she could get herself to the old woman's place. Soon, she thought, she would be dead.

She was amazed, therefore, when she heard voices on the trail above. She thought about crying out for help, but she didn't have the strength or the will. She was so thoroughly convinced that she would die that she just lay there. The people up there on the trail, whoever they were, would soon move on. But they didn't.

They had seen her from up on the trail, and some of

them made their way down to her. They straightened her broken leg and tied it to a splint, and they carried her back up to the trail. She was not much help. She was too weak. She didn't even talk to her rescuers. She drifted in and out of consciousness, and she was only aware that someone was helping her, someone was taking her somewhere. Nothing more.

Shawnee's hands were bound behind his back. He was once more a captive of the Real People. But he was confused. He had been accepted in Ijodi as the husband of the Spoiler. He was still considered an outsider by most of the people, but that was to be expected. He was, after all, a Shawnee, one of the oldest and most bitter enemies of *Ani-yunwi-ya*, the Real People. And though he lived among them, he was not really one of them.

Yet he had grown comfortable there. He had a home. He thought that perhaps these people from Kituwah did not agree with his acceptance at Ijodi. But he knew that there would be a fight when his wife and her people found out about this incident. These Paint People from Kituwah had insulted them by this action. And where was Edohi?

He had gone up on the mountaintop to meet with Edohi at Edohi's own request. And instead of finding Edohi waiting there, he had been found by these Paint People, his captors.

"What are you going to do with me?" he asked.

"You'll find out soon enough, Shawnee," said Groundhog's Brother. "Now start moving."

"Which way?" said Shawnee.

"Down the mountain. You go first. And don't try to run away. We'll be right behind you."

Shawnee knew that he wouldn't be able to get away from these men. If he tried to run down the mountain with his arms tied behind his back, he would probably only stumble and fall. Even if he could manage to keep to his feet, they would shoot him in the back. He started down the mountain trail. But then he had some hope. The trail came out at the bottom near the road, close to the town's entrance. Surely someone from Ijodi would see them. But when he had reached the road, no one had come out of the town. He stopped there to await further instructions from his captors. Groundhog's Brother put a hand on his shoulders and pushed him, turning him toward Ijodi.

"Go on," he said.

What were they doing pushing him back toward Ijodi? Didn't they know that he had friends there? That he had in-laws there? He walked on toward the town, anxious, expecting anything. No one came out of Ijodi. He walked into the passageway that led into the town, and his captors followed him. No one met them. Inside the walls, he stopped again.

"What now?" he asked.

"Keep going," said Groundhog's Brother. "Go to the town square."

Shawnee started moving toward the square. This was all very puzzling. As he got closer to the square, he could see that a crowd was gathered there. He saw Edohi and others of his Bird Clan standing there, and he saw his wife, the Spoiler, and her relatives. It looked as if they were just waiting there. Did they know about this? Had they sent him into a trap? He was thoroughly confused.

Groundhog's Brother shoved Shawnee forward until they were standing directly before Edohi. "I'm Groundhog's Brother of the Paint People from Kituwah," he said. "The Bird People say that we owe them a life. We admit nothing, but we wish to avoid further bloodshed. We have taken this Shawnee captive, and we offer him to the Bird People to replace the life that we took." Edohi turned to his mother, and Wild Hemp stepped forward and gave Shawnee a cursory glance.

"We accept," she said. "Once again, things are good between our two clans. All is even. Balance is restored. We will send word to the Bird People in all of the other towns, and no more will be said or done about this business. Now you're our guests, and you'll all stay and eat with us."

Edohi stepped toward Shawnee.

"So I'm once again your captive," said Shawnee.

Edohi moved behind Shawnee and untied the thongs that bound his wrists. Shawnee turned and looked at Edohi, puzzled still, rubbing his wrists.

"What does all this mean, Edohi?" he said. "What are you going to do with me?"

"The decision is my mother's to make," Edohi said.

"Shawnee," said Wild Hemp, "we have no need of a captive, but our clan has lost a man. We need one to replace him. If you want to be free, and if you're willing to become a Real Person, the Bird People will make you one of us. That is my decision."

Shawnee looked around to find his wife, and he saw her smiling. Edohi was a Bird Person, and he had married the daughter of the Spoiler, so Shawnee knew that his marriage would be secure. As a member of the Bird Clan, he would be allowed to have a wife of the Deer People. The whole thing slowly became clear to Shawnee. Edohi had seen a way to resolve the conflict between the Paint Clan and the Bird Clan, while offering Shawnee a real place among the Real People. For if a clan of the Real People adopted him, then he would become one of the Real People, just as if he had been born one. He glanced at Edohi with a wry smile on his face. Edohi was a clever one, he thought.

"Of course, I am willing," he said. "What you offer me is a great honor. I accept with much happiness."

"Then it will all be done," said Wild Hemp. "Come now. Let's eat."

Dancing Rabbit knew that he would have to help Edohi in his efforts to re-establish some kind of order among the Real People, but he was uncomfortable. He still felt vulnerable to possible continued vengeance against the old priesthood. Besides all that, he felt just a little useless around his sister's house in Kituwah. He had been a priest and a scribe, and both of those occupations no longer existed. He was not a great hunter, and he did not think that he could become a warrior. He had no skills. He could not make weapons or anything useful. So he had begun to think about a new profession.

He had decided that the life of a trader might be a suitable one for him. He had grown used to traveling and dealing with people of strange tongues. And, since he felt insecure at home, a life on the road was attractive. He could do nothing about it immediately, for Edohi was counting on him for help. But Edohi's plan would either work or it would not, and sooner or later, Dancing Rabbit would be free to follow his new pursuit. He decided that he would begin collecting things to take with him on his first trading expedition, and he decided that his first trip would take him south. He would not go west. He did not want to ever again see the fierce people who had made him a slave. But he would become a trader, and he would trade to the south. He began to wish that Edohi would hurry up and see him again. This other business had to be dealt with first, and Dancing Rabbit was anxious to be traveling.

Cuts-Off-Their-Heads was kept securely bound by his Suwali captors. His hands had grown numb, and he wondered if they would ever be of any use to him again. When they stopped to rest, they left him tied. When they stopped for the night to sleep, even when they ate. And they did not bother to feed him either. He figured that he was being taken back as a prisoner only to be publicly, ceremonially killed. If they wanted him for any other reason, he thought, they would feed him at least to keep him strong.

He watched closely for a chance to escape, but he saw none. He listened, but his captors spoke only their own language, and he did not understand the Suwali tongue. The Suwali warriors seldom spoke to him, and he did not bother trying to communicate with them in the trade language. He was not very good with the trade language anyway.

His chances, he decided, were not very good, yet he did not give up hope. As long as he remained alive, he would watch and wait for his chance. These Suwalis had taken his whole town by surprise. If only he could get a chance to fight with them again, he told himself, they would find a different kind of fight. He longed for that chance.

Most of the people in Ijodi, the residents and their guests, had eaten. They were lying around with full bellies, visiting, some napping, when the refugees from Taskigi arrived. Happily, there was plenty of food left from the feast, and so the weary rabble was fed. Corn Sifter seemed more dead than alive, but she was still breathing. The Spoiler took charge of the situation. She saw to it that they were all fed and any wounds were taken care of. It was late in the day, and she told them to sleep.

"The morning will be time enough to find out what has happened," she said. "In the morning, we'll gather everyone together and listen to what you have to say."

The travelers from Taskigi were grateful for that suggestion as they were practically exhausted, and so they slept. Morning found just about the entire population of Ijodi gathered at the square, waiting for the tale. The Taskigi people gathered a bit more slowly, but soon they were all there. One stood up before the crowd.

"My name is Bear Meat," he said. "I belong to the Long Hair Clan, and until recently I lived in Taskigi. All of us came from Taskigi. All except the woman with the broken leg we brought along with us. We found her on the trail hurt. She never talked to us, but we believe that we've brought her home. We believe that she lives here in your town.

"We no longer have a town. We were set upon by a large band of *Ani-Suwali*. They caught us by surprise and killed nearly everyone. We think that we are all that is left of Taskigi. The Suwalis did carry off one man with them.

I myself saw him taken. He had been knocked down and hurt or they wouldn't have captured him. It was Cuts-Off-Their-Heads, a brave fighter.

"Then from where we hid in the woods, we saw them burn our town. There is nothing left there. There is no one left but us.

"We came here to you for food and shelter and because this is the home of Edohi, the one who led the fight against the *Ani-Kutani*. We could think of no one else. Someone must lead us against these Suwalis. We came to ask Edohi."

Along with everyone else, Edohi heard the story of Taskigi with great interest. In the best of times, an attack of that nature would send the Real People off in quest of revenge. But Edohi had another thought. He almost felt guilty for thinking it, for he thought that the attack on Taskigi was perhaps a very good thing. What better way to stop the Real People from killing each other, than to set them after an enemy outside? He stood up and walked to the front of the crowd.

"Our friends and relatives from Taskigi are welcome here," he said. "Stay with us for as long as you like. You're welcome in our homes, and you're welcome to our food.

"We are all Real People. In each of our towns the same seven clans live. All of us are the children of those first Real People who came down from the Sky Vault to populate this earth.

"When the Suwali People attacked Taskigi, they attacked us all, and I am going to the country of the Suwalis to show them that they cannot insult the Real People in this cowardly way and get away with it.

"For each of our people killed, a Suwali will die, and for

Taskigi, a Suwali town will burn. I'll wait for seven days. During that time, if you want to go with me, prepare yourself for war. If any of you survivors from Taskigi want to go, we'll give you new weapons. And we'll send word to all of the other towns of Real People, so that anyone in any town who wants to join us will be able to do so. In seven days, I'll be just outside of Ijodi waiting. Join me there if you want to avenge this terrible wrong."

And the speeches went on for the rest of the day. One after another, men and women got up to speak in support of Edohi's proposal. One after another men, and a few women, declared their intent to follow Edohi to the land of the Suwali to seek revenge. Edohi listened to them all. They're coming back together, he said to himself, but with Dancing Rabbit, I'll have to act fast after this war is over to get some kind of order established. And for the first time, Edohi felt hopeful for the future.

Nine

THE SUWALI WARRIORS, with Cuts-Off-Their-Heads in tow, came to a village, and as they marched into it leading their prisoner, the people there met them and cheered them. Some of the people, men, women and children, beat Cuts-Off-Their-Heads with sticks as he passed them by. They walked all the way through the village before they stopped, allowing all who so desired to get a swipe at the helpless captive. When they finally stopped at the far edge of the village, everyone seemed to suddenly lose interest in Cuts-Off-Their-Heads. The Suwalis all ate and talked and laughed. Finally Cuts-Off-Their-Heads's captors got up to leave. Apparently this was not their village. They had just been passing through and had stopped for a rest and for food. They must be, Cuts-Off-Their-Heads thought, from a Suwali village a little farther away, a little deeper into the Suwali country. It was just as well. It would give him a little more time to think and plan. Walking out of the village and on farther into Suwali country, Cuts-Off-Their-Heads said to himself, "These Suwalis are certainly ugly people."

It was toward the end of the day when the Suwalis with Cuts-Off-Their-Heads finally reached their own village. It was not much different in appearance from a town of the Real People, although Cuts-Off-Their-Heads thought that the houses seemed to be hastily constructed. Again the men were received as triumphant returning warriors, and again Cuts-Off-Their-Heads was beaten as he was paraded through the village. Finally, the Suwalis tied him to a stake at one edge of their central plaza and stripped him naked. For a while they tormented him, and then they seemed to forget about him. He was bruised and had some small cuts and scratches, but thus far he had not been seriously hurt.

Women were cooking, and some men built a large fire in the middle of the plaza. Soon there was feasting and dancing and singing, and Cuts-Off-Their-Heads could tell that some sort of victory celebration was in progress. He wondered if his death would be a part of the ceremony, but he knew very little about the Suwali People, only that they were his enemies.

Suwali men danced in a circle around the fire, leaping and yelling triumphantly. In a wider circle outside of the men's circle, Suwali women danced. They were much more subdued, even sedate, and one of the women, as she passed the stake to which he was tied, glanced at Cuts-Off-Their-Heads. Her large brown eyes rolled up to look at him, then looked away. It was only an instant, but Cuts-Off-Their-Heads was totally enamored. He tried to recall how she looked as she moved on around the circle, moved away from him, out of his sphere of vision, but he could only recall the eyes. He waited anxiously for her to come around again, and at last she did, but this time she did not look. He studied her shape from behind, memorized her clothing, watched her long, loose hair sway from side to side as she danced. And then Cuts-Off-Their-Heads knew that he not only must escape from these people, but he must also take her with him. He had to have this Suwali woman for his own.

"Smoke with me," said Gone-in-the-Water, and he handed the pipe to his guest, Edohi. Edohi took the pipe, puffed four times and handed it back to the old man.

"Uncle, I have to talk to you some more," said Edohi. "I'm not sure what to do."

"You're lucky then," said the old man. "I almost died."

"Were you ill?" asked Edohi.

"No. I had a woman come to me for help. Someone was doing something to her. I gave her something to help, and I got weak. I think my spirit was fighting with the spirit of the other conjurer. But I got better, so I think the other one must be dead, or nearly so."

"Who was it?" said Edohi. "Do you know?"

Gone-in-the-Water puffed on his pipe. He glanced slyly toward Edohi.

"What do you want to talk about?" he said.

"The Suwalis destroyed one of our towns," Edohi said.

"Taskigi," said the conjurer. "Yes. I heard."

"We're planning to attack them in return. It seemed to me that it should be done."

Gone-in-the-Water nodded his head slowly as he sucked on his pipe.

"It's proper," he said. "A life for a life. A town for a town."

"I thought, too," said Edohi, "that killing Suwalis would keep our people from killing each other—at least for a while."

"Yes," said the old man. "That's also a good thought. You're probably right. There's nothing so good for peace at home as a good war with one's neighbors."

"But when we return," Edohi said, "we still have the other problem. Dancing Rabbit will help with the ceremonies, I think, but what do we do between the ceremonies? How do we keep order from day to day?"

"Edohi," said Gone-in-the-Water, "everything exists in pairs. There is day and night, light and dark, winter and summer. There is life and death, and there is male and female. There is peace and there is war. Below us is the underworld, and above us is the world at the Seventh Height. Everything in pairs of opposites. This is perhaps the most important thing that we can know."

Edohi sat silent for a moment thinking. The old man calmly smoked his pipe.

"I understand what you've said," Edohi said, "but how do I make use of that knowledge? It seems as if our people have all gone crazy."

"No. They haven't gone crazy. They've just lost their balance. The *Ani-Kutani* were our leaders," Gone-in-the-Water said. "They are no more. You killed them. We need leaders to maintain order, but we do not want leaders with so much power. We need to have some control over our leaders. And we do not need leaders with power over all of the Real People."

"You mean, leaders in each town?" asked Edohi.

"Of course."

"Each town should have its own priests?"

"And more," said Gone-in-the-Water. "There is peace and there is war. There are men and there are women. There is light and dark, day and night, earth and sky, fire and water, hot and cold.

"Go home now, Edohi, and get ready for your war against the Suwali people, but when the war is over, think about what I've just told you. Everything exists in pairs. And think about yourself, too."

Edohi walked away from Gone-in-the-Water's house not knowing quite what to think. He wasn't sure how the information about everything being made of pairs of opposites was supposed to help him solve the problems of the Real People, and he was also wondering what the old man had meant by his final charge: "And think about yourself, too."

"Think about myself," he said in a quiet voice as he walked along. "Think about myself. Everything exists in pairs. Why, the sly old fox was telling me that I need another woman."

And then Edohi thought about Sohi, and he realized that he was able for the first time since the death of his first wife to think about another without a terrible pain in his heart. Perhaps the time was right, and Gone-in-the-Water knew it. Gone-in-the-Water knew most things. Well, he would talk to his uncle Hemp Carrier about it, and then he would talk to his mother. He thought that Sohi would be agreeable to the idea, and he knew that his mother-in-law, the Spoiler, would approve. It was no secret that she had more than once expressed the opinion that this marriage should take place.

So he would get himself another wife. He had just decided. And the wedding would take place—when? After he had returned from attacking the Suwalis? Or should he resolve these other problems first? Bring harmony back to the Real People? But he had no idea how long that would take to accomplish. Hemp Carrier would help him make that decision. Or his mother.

As Edohi walked between the walls to go into Ijodi, he felt better than he had felt in a long time, perhaps better than he had felt since his childhood. The problems were still out there ahead of him, but he thought that he was beginning to see their solutions. He had a feeling that things would all work out for the best. And it was a good feeling. But he had to think about that business of the pairs and how they might relate to restoring the harmony. Perhaps Dancing Rabbit could help him with that.

In front of her house just outside the walls of Kituwah, Breaks-Things-Up squatted in the dirt before a small fire and ate soup from a wooden bowl with a wooden spoon. The soup was hot, and the spoon was large and thick and somewhat awkward to use. As she slurped at it, soup dripped from the spoon onto the ground where it formed a little puddle, and soup ran down the old woman's chin.

Her skin was wrinkled, but the wrinkles had the look of deep grooves sliced in hard leather. There was nothing brittle or weak-seeming about Breaks-Things-Up. Her hair, streaked with gray, hung long and loose over her shoulders, and it was tangled and matted and dirty. Her whole appearance was generally unkempt, terribly casual and unconcerned.

An arbor extended off one end of her tiny house, and from its poles dangled a variety of plants in various stages of drying. Under the arbor was an array of pots and mortars, some full, some partly filled with herbs and roots and leaves. A skunk skin dangled from one pole, buzzard feathers from another. And over all hung a slightly fetid odor, a smell like the smell of death, but just a little sweeter.

She finished her soup and stood up, not quite straight. Her back had a permanent crook, and she leaned on a staff as she walked.

"That woman should have come back by now, I thought," she mumbled, talking, perhaps, to herself. "I wonder why she has not."

She hobbled toward her door, but she stopped abruptly and winced as if from a sharp and unexpected pain.

"Ah," she said. It seemed to pass, and she took another step. "Ah." This time her voice was louder, her face more twisted with the pain. She bent forward even more than her natural stoop and dropped her bowl and spoon as she clutched at her guts with her one free hand. Her other hand gripped the staff tightly to hold her up, and it trembled, and her body wavered slightly from side to side. She took a deep breath, and then she howled with pain and anger and dropped down hard to her knees.

"Ah," she said. "There's something in there. Someone has put something in there."

She fell forward on her hands, and her body convulsed as she made dry, raspy heaving sounds, but nothing came out. Only saliva dripped from her wrinkled old lips.

"Who?" she said. "Who has done this to me?"

She heaved some more, still in vain. Whatever it was, it would not come out. And then she felt it move, and then she knew. It was the very thing she herself had sent out to kill that other woman, and someone with more power than she had sent it back, and it was in her now. And she knew that there was no defense. It was too late. She writhed and twisted with the pain, and with a final growl like that of some dying animal, she collapsed into a lifeless heap between her fire and her house.

In the Suwali village, the festivities lasted long into the night. Now and then Cuts-Off-Their-Heads drifted into sleep, but when he did, a Suwali would come along and slap his face to wake him up. Other than that, they left him alone. At last they quit and headed for their houses, and Cuts-Off-Their-Heads watched closely to see where the Suwali woman with the big eyes went. And he saw her, and he took note of the house. He would remember it. He would not leave without her.

But how would he escape? They had tied his wrists together in front of him, then pulled his arms up over his head and tied them high up on the pole. But nothing else was tied. His feet were free. He twisted himself around until he was facing the pole. The change tightened the bonds around his wrists, but he could still flex his fingers. He gripped the pole as well as he could, and then he began to climb with his feet. He was glad they had taken away his moccasins, for his bare feet gripped the pole well. His feet were close to his hands, and then he wondered what he would do next. He had thought that perhaps he would be able to slip the thongs that bound his wrists up over the top of the pole, but it was taking all of his strength to just cling to the pole that way. He could do no more. He was about to give it up and crawl back down when he felt the pole tilt just a little with his weight. He looked around, and he saw no Suwalis out anywhere in the open. They were all inside asleep. He began to throw his weight back and forth and rock the pole, and each time he did, the pole leaned farther over, his back dropped closer to the ground.

Then it came loose and dropped suddenly, and he landed on his back with a thud. The wind was knocked out of his lungs, and he lay there for a moment catching his breath. At last he rolled to one side, coming out from under the pole, and he slipped the thongs off the end, and he was free.

His wrists were still tied together, though, and there was the woman. He had to think quickly. He could afford no mistakes.

Ten

CUTS-OFF-THEIR-HEADS stood for a moment in a low crouch, looking around to see if his movements had been detected by any Suwali. He saw no one, heard nothing but the night sounds of birds and bugs. The village dogs had gotten used to his presence there and did not bark. They apparently did not know that he was supposed to be tied to the stake.

He was free from the stake, but his wrists were still tied, and he was unarmed and naked and alone in the middle of the Suwali village and deep in Suwali country. He knew that he should run. He should run into the woods and get as far from his enemies as he could and worry later about freeing his wrists. But he did not run. He did not run because he wanted the woman. He looked toward the house he had seen her go into, but he knew that he could not simply go in there and get her. There were others in there, her parents, he supposed, and he was hampered by his bound wrists.

He began walking, slowly and cautiously, and he peered into the first house he came to. Several people slept in there. He moved to the next house, and he found it, too, crowded with sleeping Suwalis. Thus he moved from one house to another until he had gone all the way down the row and was coming back along the row of facing houses. Soon he would reach the house in which she slept.

He was just two doors away from her house when he saw the knife. It was inside, on the ground, within easy reach of a sleeping Suwali man. It was also within easy reach of Cuts-Off-Their-Heads. He had only to kneel close to the house and stretch his arms through the doorway. He knelt, and the noise of his own heartbeat seemed loud to him in the still night. His own breaths came raspy and loud to his ears, and he thought that he would surely wake the sleeping man and perhaps even the others in the house. He began to reach for the knife, and he saw that his arms were trembling, and he felt the beads of sweat running down his forehead. And he clutched the knife tight in his right hand, but its hilt was slippery in the wet grasp of his sweating palm. The Suwali man stirred in his sleep, and Cuts-Off-Their-Heads felt his own heart thump irregularly in his chest. Slowly, he withdrew the knife from the house, and slowly he stood up.

Triumphant and relieved, he walked around behind the row of houses a safe distance to work with the knife at his bonds. Soon he was free. He flexed his fingers and rubbed his wrists. Then he untied the knots from the rawhide thongs he had cut off his wrists and straightened the rope. He had a short piece about as long as his arm and a longer one almost the length of his leg. He rolled them up and slung them over his shoulder, and he moved back around to the front of the houses.

A little bolder than before, but still cautious, he walked to the woman's house. For a moment he stood outside the door. He crouched and looked inside. At first he could see only four forms asleep on the floor. Then he found her. She was lying against the side wall to his left. To get to her, he would have to go inside and walk past her father, who was lying against the front wall to the left of the doorway.

He did not want to kill anyone in this house. The woman would not ever want him if he had killed her father or her mother. And there was a young man in the house, a brother, he assumed, for he slept against the wall opposite the young woman. So how could he get to her without waking everyone else in the house? And if he did rouse anyone else in the process of getting to her, how could he then get her out without killing someone? He thought about clapping a hand over her mouth and holding the point of the knife to her throat, but that would not assure her absolute silence. If she was brave or foolish, she might cry out in spite of the threat. He decided that he would have to wait for a better time. He would have to try to catch her alone. And that meant that he would have to stay around for a while and watch the village and wait for the right opportunity. He had already resolved that he would not leave without her.

He knew that he was pushing his luck by remaining in the village longer, but he poked around a little more, stealing a blanket, a ball-headed warclub and some food. Then he left the village, headed back the way from which he had come. He was careful to leave a trail that the

Suwalis would easily follow. They would automatically as-
sume that he was headed for home, and he intended to do
everything he could to reinforce that notion. He walked
away a good part of what was left of the night, and when
he found himself paralleling a small stream, he walked
into the water. Then he backtracked, and when he came
out of the water again, he was careful to conceal his trail.
He made his way into the woods and back toward the
village he had just escaped from. If his ruse worked, the
Suwalis would think that he had escaped them and was on
his way back to the land of the Real People. They would
not look for him in the woods close to their own village.

Gone-in-the-Water came awake on his own cot in his
own house. For a moment he thought that everything was
normal, but as his head cleared he became puzzled. He
tried to think, but he could only recall that he had
stretched out on the ground in exhaustion there near the
place in the woods where he had gone to harvest *jola
gayunli*, the ancient tobacco. He could not remember getting up and walking back home. But here he was in his
own house. He was confused.

"I've gotten too old," he said to himself. "I do things,
and I don't remember them. I should stop living so long."

He sat up on the cot and rubbed his rheumy old eyes
with the backs of his bony, leathery hands. Then he
blinked and looked around the room. He was still feeling
somewhat befuddled. Then he heard a voice.

"What?" he said. "What's that? What do you mean?
Why am I an ungrateful old fool? Oh. You did it? You and
Ugly? I was collapsed there in the woods, and you
brought me back here, did you? You didn't think I could

make it back by myself? Ha. I would have slept awhile and then got up and walked home. I'm not so old I can't walk home. Have you fixed us anything to eat? No? You were waiting for me to wake up and do it? I should have known. I always have to fix our food. All right. All right. I'll fix us something, and then I want to go into town and see what's happening there. I'm curious about those two women. And I wonder about Edohi and what he's doing. There's too much going on right now for me to sleep the rest of my life away. Fetch me that bowl over there, Noisy. I'm wasting time."

Edohi rose early on the morning of the seventh day. For four days he had fasted. He should have slept on ashes from the sacred fire, he knew, but all the fires had gone out. There had been no one to kindle a sacred fire since the killing of the priests. Still, he had prepared himself as best he could, as best he knew how, for going to war. He painted his right side black from shoulder to foot, and on his left forehead, left breast, left upper arm and left thigh, he painted seven red stripes. Running from just below his left knee to just above his left foot, he painted a wavy red line, like a snake. He donned breechclout and moccasins, and he tied a strip of eel skin around each wrist. To his waist in the back he attached a gray fox tail, and he tied four white egret feathers to the long, flowing hair of his scalplock. Finally he took up his warclub. It was wooden and ball-headed, but into the ball was set a sharp flint blade.

He left his mother's house and walked to the edge of the town. As he emerged on the outside of the passageway between the overlapping ends of the fence, he saw the crowd gathered there waiting for him, and he felt a surge of pride.

There was his uncle, Hemp Carrier, and beside him stood the Shawnee. Bear Meat and a few others from Taskigi were there, newly armed by the residents of Ijodi. And Groundhog's Brother was there with a group from Kituwah. And there were more. Edohi knew most of them, but there were a few who were strangers to him, people from Kituwah or Taskigi or from some other town. It was a good army, Edohi thought. They should easily accomplish their task.

He was about to lead them on their way when he saw the old man approaching. In his left hand, Gone-in-the-Water carried a clay pot from which a thin wisp of smoke trailed, and in his right, he carried a feather from the wing of an eagle. He walked straight to Edohi, and with the feather, he wafted the smoke toward the war leader. When he had done, he walked among the others and did the same to them. Then he turned toward Edohi once more.

"Go your way," he said, "and return victorious."

Edohi waved an arm and started walking toward the Suwali land. The others followed him. Gone-in-the-Water watched until they were out of sight.

"I knew there was a reason for me to be here this morning," he said. Then he went on inside the town.

It was still early, but people were beginning to stir. They had been awakened by the men preparing to go to war. Some few people were going to the river to start their day, but most were just milling about the town. Gone-in-the-Water did his best to avoid them, but he had to speak to a

few as he made his way through the town. At last he came
to the spot he wanted. There was a crumbling, abandoned
house, and he sat in front of it just at its doorway. From
there he could see the front of the houses of both Moleskin and Corn Sifter. He placed the smoldering pot on
the ground beside him and held the feather in front of his
chest. Then he settled down to watch.

In a short while, Moleskin came out of her house. She
stood for a moment, looking toward the east where the
sky was just beginning to show pink above the tree line.
Then Corn Sifter came out of her house.

" *'Siyo*," she said. "*Tohiju?*"

" *'Siyo*," said Moleskin, looking over toward her neigh-
bor and recent enemy. "I'm just fine today. Thank you."

"Are you going to the river?" asked Corn Sifter.

"Are you?"

"Yes."

"Then I'll go with you, if that's all right," said Moleskin.

"Yes," said Corn Sifter. "Of course it's all right. I don't
like to go alone."

Watching the two women walk together toward the
river, the old man slowly nodded his head. Of course, he
knew, they could be feigning friendliness toward one another, but he didn't think so. He felt, at his advanced age,
he could tell when one was not sincere, and he believed
the trouble between those two to be over. He had done
his job well, and it was good. And it was a good sign in
general. These feuds could, after all, be resolved. Edohi
had resolved one such feud by making use of the Shawnee, and now everything seemed to be all right between
these two women. Perhaps things would all work out in

just as satisfactory a way. Perhaps Gone-in-the-Water after all would live to see the Real People living with one another in harmony again. It was the only thing left that he yet wanted out of life.

Cuts-Off-Their-Heads was almost out of food. He could perhaps kill some small game in the woods without being detected by the Suwalis, but he would not have been able to cook it without giving away his presence by the smoke of his fire. So he contented himself with the food he had stolen from the Suwali village and with what plant food he could find growing there in his new neighborhood. He had found himself a small cave in the woods near the stream that ran by the village, and in that he kept his dwindling supply of food and his blanket. He slept there, too, but during the daylight, he spent most of his time watching the Suwali village.

The woman for whom he watched was a delight to his eyes whenever she appeared, and he found himself longing for her touch more and more. Sooner or later, he knew, she would have to venture away from the village alone, not far, perhaps, but far enough for him to make his move. She would go for water, or she would go to the woods to relieve herself, or something. But then, he told himself, it would have to be soon. He would be out of food in another day or two. Of course, he could sneak back into the village at night and steal some more, but he did not really want to do that. He didn't want to do anything that might arouse the suspicions of the Suwalis. His original trick had worked, it seemed. Some of the men had followed his trail out of town the morning after his escape. They had come back later, obviously disappointed. If he stole anything more from them, they might get the idea that he was still lurking around, and they might begin to search for him again. He didn't want that.

He wanted only to watch quietly and secretly until the woman made one small mistake which would allow him to capture her, to grab her and keep her quiet and to escape with her without having to fight with anyone. He could get hurt in a fight, and then it would be more difficult to get home with her, or worse yet, she could be hurt. That was the last thing he wanted to happen. He had to be careful, and he would not have time to plan. When the opportunity presented itself, he would have to act fast.

So he continued to watch, and he resented more and more everything that caused him to abandon his watch, even for a brief moment. The opportunity for which he waited could come at any time, and it might last but a few blinks of an eye.

Eleven

DANCING RABBIT had accumulated almost enough wares to make a trading trip worthwhile. Soon he would be ready to try his new occupation. He would load up as much as he could carry on his back and head south, as far south as he could go. The Real People knew about the people to the south, and Dancing Rabbit had a pretty good idea of the kinds of goods he would be able to return home with. There would be dangers, of course, but he did not think that the dangers would be great. They would certainly not compare with the dangers of his trip to the West and back, and, he thought with a certain sense of irony, they might not even compare to the present dangers at home. He was beginning to look forward anxiously to the start of this trip.

But he was also beginning to think of an added element to his plans. As Gnat's maternal uncle, he was responsible for the training and discipline of the boy. Discipline had never been a problem. Gnat was a good boy who had early on developed a strong sense of the rights of others as well as of his own responsibilities. But now it was time to be thinking of training for the boy's future. What role would he fill as a man? Gnat had already just about mastered the writing, but that would have to remain a secret. The preservation of the old sacred symbols with which one could mark down his own words had become, since the slaughter of the priests, a very private matter. It certainly could not be Gnat's public occupation.

And Dancing Rabbit knew that he was not suited to train his nephew as a hunter or a warrior or a doctor. Why, then, he asked himself, did he not take Gnat along with him on this trip? Why not train the boy to become a trader? That should be a good occupation for them both. Gnat was almost always at the heels of Dancing Rabbit anyway. The only problem would be convincing Walnut, his sister, the boy's mother. She might not like the idea of her son's leaving home for such a long trip at such an early age. She would worry about his safety. She would miss him. She would probably not allow it at all. In spite of that, Dancing Rabbit decided, he would ask her, and if necessary, he would argue with her and try his best to convince her that it was a good plan.

He realized that he had begun to leave Edohi and the problems of the Real People out of his plans, and when he thought about Edohi, he felt a little guilty. But he had never really wanted that responsibility anyway, had not sought it. He had, at best, he reminded himself, reluctantly agreed to help. He decided that as soon as he was ready, as soon as his sister agreed to allow Gnat to go with him, he would pack up and get out. Maybe everything would be resolved at home by the time they returned.

. . . .

When Edohi thought that he had crossed into Suwali country, he sent Groundhog's Brother ahead to scout, and he and the other warriors moved ahead more slowly. The general plan was for the Real People to come upon the Suwalis by surprise. He did not want the opposite to happen. They had not gone very far before Groundhog's Brother returned. Edohi called a halt.

"There is a village up ahead," said Groundhog's Brother. "It's a small village. We can take it easily."

"Did you see any Suwalis outside of the village?" asked Edohi.

"No."

"How far ahead of us is this village?"

Groundhog's Brother pointed ahead on the narrow, uphill trail to the horizon.

"When we get up there," he said, "we'll be looking down on it. But it's a long run from the top of the hill there to the village across an open field. When we can see them, they will be able to see us, too."

"Let's go on up there then," said Edohi, "but let's not show ourselves yet. We'll camp there for the night, and just as the sun peeks out in the morning to show her first light, we'll attack.

"But there's something I want to say before we go into this fight. I don't like making war on women and children. Kill the warriors and burn the village. That's all."

"But the Suwalis killed our women and children at Taskigi," protested one of the survivors of that unhappy town.

"We are *Ani-yunwi-ya*. We are not Suwalis," said Edohi. "Let's not act like them."

"What if the Suwali women come at us with weapons?" asked Groundhog's Brother.

"If they try to fight us with weapons, then they are warriors," said Edohi. "Now. Do you all agree to this?"

No one said anything, and so Edohi knew that he had won the debate. He knew that some might not really agree with his decision, but disagreement unexpressed did not count.

"Come on then," he said, and they followed him up the trail toward the ridge ahead.

He saw her from his hiding place on the wooded hillside. She walked out of her house, and she had under her arm a large gourd vessel, a vessel one would use to hold water. His heart pounded with anticipation. She might be going to the stream, and the stream was far enough from the Suwali village to give him his chance. He watched, ready to spring into action. She was walking in the right direction through the village. She spoke to people as she passed them by, but she kept going in the direction of the stream with her gourd vessel under her arm. He stood up and moved in her direction. Then he hesitated, his high hopes suddenly dashed.

She had stopped and was talking to another young woman. She stood there alone in the street while the other woman went inside a house. In a moment the second woman reappeared carrying a water gourd of her own, and the two women walked together toward the stream. He continued to watch them, but now without hope. He could still take her, he thought, if they went to the right part of the stream, if they went to a spot where they would not be easily observed from the village. But even so, he might have to hurt or even kill the other woman. He did not want to do that.

He had no desire to kill a woman. He especially had no desire to do anything in front of the woman he wanted that might tend to horrify her or make him hateful in her eyes. She would hate him enough for stealing her away from her own people, but he would work to overcome that hatred. And he did not want to make that chore any more difficult than it would already be.

But his thoughts were racing ahead of him. He did not even have the woman yet. He wondered how long he would have to wait for another chance. He decided to make his move. He worked his way through the woods to a spot close to the stream. In doing so, he had lost sight of the women.

The only way he could possibly relocate them was to take a chance on exposing himself. But he had no choice, he thought, and so he stepped out of the cover of the woods to look downstream. There they were. They were both kneeling beside the water, their gourds in the running stream. He stepped back into the woods and began to make his way through them, moving closer to the women. He would be able to remain concealed until he was close enough to run only a few steps and grab the woman by surprise. He had no plan beyond that. He would rush out and grab the woman. He would brandish the knife he had stolen in an effort to frighten the other woman away. If that failed to work, well, he would just wait and see what would happen, and he would react to it then.

He moved slowly, being careful to be as quiet in the woods as possible. Then he was as close as he could get.

He was about to rush out of his cover and attack, when the other woman stood up with her gourd. She said something. The other answered. Then the second woman turned and started walking back toward the village. He could scarcely believe his luck.

The woman he wanted was left alone. Her gourd, filled with water, was sitting there on the ground beside the stream. She stood up, stepped out of her moccasins and dropped her short skirt to the ground. She was naked there beside the stream, and Cuts-Off-Their-Heads was nearly overcome by her beauty. He fought off an urge to just stay there hidden and watch her, but he knew that he had to act fast or not at all. The other one was out of sight at last, and he sprang from his hiding place.

He was on her before she could shout. At the last instant, she heard his approach, and she turned to face him, but he put his left arm around her shoulders and pulled her close to him, his right hand clapped firmly over her mouth. She struggled, but he was too strong for her. There was nothing she could do.

But neither was there anything he could do, not the way they were, two naked bodies pressed close together. His ropes were slung over his shoulder, and the knife was there hanging from the ropes. He could threaten her with the knife to make her do what he wanted, but in order to get the knife, he would have to release her with one of his hands. If he used his left hand to get the knife, she could run. If he used his right, she could shout. He couldn't decide what to do. Then he remembered the trade language. It was worth a try.

"I don't want to hurt you," he said, using the jargon.

She looked at him, seemingly surprised by the communication.

"Do you understand me?" he asked.

She nodded an affirmative answer.

"Then pick up your moccasins and your skirt," he said. "You're coming with me."

He maintained his grip on her, but allowed her to bend enough to do as he had said. Then he moved with her, awkwardly, toward the semi-safety of the woods. It was slow and awkward moving with her like that, but they were still close enough to the village for a shout to be heard. He had to keep her quiet. He continued the clumsy walk through the woods.

At last he felt that perhaps he had gotten them far enough away to take a chance. He stopped, and he spoke to her again.

"If you promise not to shout, I'll take my hand away from your mouth," he said in the jargon. "Do you promise?"

She nodded.

"All right," he said. "I'm going to take my hand away, but if you shout, I'll have to hurt you to keep you quiet. I don't want to hurt you, but I will if you shout."

"What do you want with me?" she said, and there was a hard edge of hatred to her voice. He noticed, too, that her command of the trade language was even better than his own.

"Never mind that for now," he said. "Put on your skirt and your moccasins."

She dressed herself quickly, and she shot him a look which betrayed both hatred and confusion. He took her by the arms and turned her around, pulling her hands behind her back. Then he tied her wrists together with the short piece of rope. He took the longer piece and tied it around her neck, not tight enough to choke her, but in too small a loop for her to pull it over her head. The other end of the rope he tied around his own left wrist.

"Come on," he said, and he started walking deeper into the woods. His plan was to stay well in the woods until he was a safe distance away from her village. Then he would move back closer to the trail. Even then he would stay in the woods as much as possible. He would try to stay off the trail until they had passed well beyond the other village, the one he and his captors had stopped in on their way. From there the way should be clear, and the going should be easier.

It was late evening when he stopped in a small clearing in the woods.

"We'll rest here," he said.

"Now will you tell me what you want with me?" she asked.

"Yes," he said. "I want you for my woman. I knew it when I first saw you, when you danced by me that night I was tied in your village. I saw you, and I wanted you. I've never wanted another woman so much. I've never felt this way about a woman."

"You don't even know me," she said.

"I will," he said.

"We're enemies."

"No," he said. "I'm not your enemy. I could never be your enemy."

"I will always be your enemy. I'll kill you when I get a chance, and I'll never be your woman. You'll have to take me by force if you want me."

"I won't do that," said Cuts-Off-Their-Heads. "I'll be good to you. You'll get to know me, and one day you'll want me, too."

"Ha," she said. "That will never happen."

"I'm called Cuts-Off-Their-Heads," he said. "I come from a town called Taskigi, but it doesn't exist anymore. The ones who captured me destroyed it. I belong to the Long Hair Clan of the Real People. What do they call you?"

She set her mouth in a pout and glared at him.

"If you don't tell me, I'll make up something to call you," he said.

"Call me anything you like," she said. "I don't care what you call me."

"Well, we've rested here long enough."

Cuts-Off-Their-Heads stood up and tugged a little on the rope, but the woman didn't move.

"I'm hungry," she said.

"We'll eat tomorrow," he said. "Tonight we travel. Come on."

Reluctantly, she stood up, and she followed him as he continued his way through the woods.

Twelve

THE SUN had just provided the first early indications of the beginning of her daily journey across the underside of the Sky Vault, when the sleeping people of the Suwali border village were awakened by a loud, clamorous reverberation like that of a large flock of angry turkeys racing toward them. It took them a startled moment to wake up and clear their heads and another moment of uncertainty to sort out the sounds and realize that it was not real turkeys they were hearing and finally to recall that the war cry of the Real People was an imitation of the cry of a turkey. Those brief moments of confused hesitation were their downfall.

Many of them had come rushing out of their houses unarmed, curious, looking to see what they could see. A few had come out armed. All were overwhelmed by the swift and fierce attack of Edohi's band of Real People. Some of the men who had emerged from their houses without weapons were cut down as they were, unarmed, surprised and defenseless. Others had managed to duck back inside their houses when they realized what was happening. Then they grabbed the nearest weapons they could lay their hands on and came back out to fight. By then the Real People were upon them, and though armed, they were beaten down as they came out of their doors.

Hemp Carrier bashed in the skull of a Suwali woman who ran at him brandishing a warclub, and a man from Taskigi in his rage ran his spear through an unarmed Suwali woman from the back as she ran, but other than that, no women were killed. The rest of them fled, and the warriors of the Real People allowed them to go, living up to their agreement with Edohi.

Almost as soon as the fighting started, mothers grabbed up their small children and ran, and larger children ran on their own. Old men and old women hobbled away toward the safety of the woods as fast as their brittle bones would carry them. No children were killed and no old people. But the men of fighting age who stayed and fought, fought to the death. Edohi's furious band killed them all. The slaughter was swift, brutal and merciless. The Suwali warriors had outnumbered the attackers when the fight began, but the attack had been so sudden and unexpected, so ferocious, that the numbers mattered but little in the end.

And at last it was over, as suddenly as it had begun. Blood-splattered, Edohi stood in the middle of the conquered Suwali village. The only life left there was the bloody and still furious band of Real People. Bodies of Suwali men were scattered here and there in grotesque attitudes of violent death, among them the bodies of the two women. All of the other women, all of the children, all of the old people had fled in terror to the nearby woods for safety. Then came the wild and raucous shouts and whoops of triumph and elation. Edohi, not deigning to join this spontaneous celebration, remained aloof and calmly waited for the ebullient behavior of his band to subside. Then, finally, when the cacophony began to subside and things were nearly quiet, he spoke out again.

"Search all the houses," he said. "Take anything you want. The rest will be destroyed before we leave this place."

The victorious warriors, their eyes still wild from fresh carnage, ran up and down the streets, in and out of houses. They gathered knives, warclubs, spears, bows and arrows, pots and baskets, blankets, robes, some food, and then Edohi called a halt and spoke again.

"Now," he said, "set fire to all the houses, and then we'll go home to let our friends and families know what we've accomplished here today."

As the triumphant band of Real People turned their backs on the scene of battle and walked toward home, their arms laden with booty, the village behind them crackled as hungry flames licked at the sides of houses and raced across the roofs, sending clouds of black smoke billowing up into the sky. Where there had been a village, there would soon be none. There would be nothing but dead bodies and piles of ashes. The wretched Suwalis would think hard before attacking another town of the Real People.

Cuts-Off-Their-Heads and the Suwali woman saw the smoke and, as they moved closer, the flames. It had already been the plan of Cuts-Off-Their-Heads to circle wide around the border village to avoid any contact with Suwalis. But the sight of the flames caused him to pause and reconsider. He knew it was the border town that was burning, and he surmised that his own people had done the deed in retaliation for the destruction of Taskigi. The woman, he thought, had probably figured all this out as well, but they did not speak of it.

Cuts-Off-Their-Heads thought about going straight into the burning village. Perhaps his own people would still be there, and he could join them for the trip back to his own country. But if they were gone already, and if he headed for the village, then he would be likely to run into refugees who would be very angry indeed, and who, having run away from their attackers, would like nothing better than to come across a lone and naked representative of that same group. The other reason he would have liked to go on into the village was to see whether or not there was anything left unburned which he might use for a breechclout or a robe. He would have liked some moccasins, too. He was getting a little tired of wandering around entirely unclothed.

"Well," said the woman, and her impatient voice surprised and startled him a little, "what are you going to do now?"

"I'm considering what to do," he said.

"I'm hungry," she said. "You promised me food today."

Food, he thought. That was another thing he might find yet in the village. So he decided that he would go to the village after all. He would go, but he would still circle wide, as he had planned, until he had come even with the site of the village but off to one side. That way, he would

probably bypass any refugees, who would most likely be
fleeing deeper into their own territory, probably into the
very village from which he himself had escaped.

"Come on," he said.

It was midday before he reached the site of the burned-
out village. The woman was walking along behind him,
still glaring at him with hate-filled eyes. They had not
encountered any refugees from the village. They did not
see anyone alive in the ruins, not Suwalis, not Real People. They stood for a moment on the edge of the woods,
staring at smoldering ash heaps that had been houses, at
the bloody and contorted bodies lying about here and
there.

"It's your people who have done this," said the woman.

"Yes," he said, "but they had reason. That is what your
people did to my town when I was captured. Come on."

Looking around, leading his sullen captive by her leash,
he moved slowly and tentatively toward the remains of the
village. There was still no sign of life. The people who
had fled the village were probably long gone, and they
would not be likely to return until they were reasonably
certain that those who had attacked them were well on
their way back home. Yet he remained cautious, and he
took his time getting across the clearing. The woman was
impatient and ran out ahead of him, pulling on her leash,
but he held her back. He understood her impulse. It was,
after all, a village of her own people. She probably had
friends and relatives living there.

Once down in the village, Cuts-Off-Their-Heads
stopped at one of the bodies and stripped it of breechclout
and moccasins and dressed himself. Then he glanced at

the Suwali woman, and he could see that, though trying to restrain herself, perhaps because of his presence, she appeared to be grief-stricken. He recalled the Suwali attack on Taskigi and told himself that he was glad of what had happened here. Yet he felt compassion for this woman. He watched her for a moment, then untied the rope from his wrist and dropped it to the ground.

"Mourn as you will," he said. "I'll search for food for us both."

He left her alone for the rest of the afternoon, and she did not run away. He was a little surprised at that, although he was never too far away from her, and he watched her closely. She could tell that, and she might also have known that if she had tried to run, he could have caught her easily. Or she might have felt the need to stay and grieve over some of her fallen people there. Whatever her reason, she stayed, and he left her to herself.

It was early evening before he decided to approach her again. She had knelt beside several of the bodies and moaned and keened, but she was quiet now, subdued, solemn. She was on her knees at the edge of the village staring off toward the woods. He had found some food that had not been burned beyond use, and he carried it to where she knelt. He sat down beside her and placed the food on the ground between them.

"Here," he said. "Eat."

She was no longer in a mood to eat, but she was still hungry, so she ate a little. He, too, ate but little. For a while they sat side by side in awkward silence. Then she picked up the loose end of the rope and handed it to him. She was ready to go.

"I suppose now you'll always hate me," he said, holding the rope end loosely in his hand. "That's not what I wanted."

She did not respond. She only sat and stared. He turned his head and looked at her. She was remarkably beautiful, he thought, the most beautiful woman he had ever seen, and she looked profoundly sad at just that moment. He turned away and looked back over the so recently devastated village behind them. His hand relaxed, and he dropped the rope to the ground.

"I want you," he said, "more than I've ever wanted a woman. I had decided that I would die before I'd return home without you, but I won't force you to stay with me. If you stay on the trail, it won't take you too long to get back home. Those of my people who did this here today are gone. They are well on their way back home. It will be safe enough now between here and your village for you to travel alone. You're free. Go on."

She looked at him unbelieving, but he sat still, and now it was he who stared listlessly ahead. She stood up, but she did not go. Still he did not move. She untied the noose from around her neck and tossed the length of rope aside. And still he did not move. She turned with a haughty toss of her head and started walking back toward her home, but she had only taken a few steps when she stopped abruptly and turned to face him again. He was still sitting there, still staring at the road that led toward his own land. She hesitated a moment, and then she spoke to him.

"You'd better go," she said. "Some of my people might come around soon. If you wait too long, they'll find you here."

"It doesn't matter," he said.

"You only have a knife. You won't be able to defend yourself if they catch you here."

He made no response. She started again to leave, and again she stopped and turned back toward him. She stood staring at his back, puzzled, exasperated, suddenly undecided, and a moment later, as if he sensed her continued presence, he looked over his shoulder to see her standing there.

"Why are you still here?" he asked.

"My name is Rising Fawn," she said. "I don't want them to kill you."

Incredulous, he stood up slowly, turning to face her.

"All right," he said. "I'll go now. Then you can go as well."

"Good," she said. "And so I'll go with you."

Cuts-Off-Their-Heads was astonished. He thought that she might be teasing him. He thought that he had not heard her correctly. What he thought he had heard her say seemed too good to be true.

"You'll go with me?" he said.

She smiled, just a little smile, and nodded her head.

"Yes," she said. "I'll go with you."

"But I meant what I said to you. I set you free. You can go home now. I won't try to stop you."

"If I'm free, I can go with you if I choose. Don't you want me anymore?"

"Oh, yes," he said. "Of course I do. I've told you how I feel."

"Well then, let's go," she said, "before someone shows up here."

Cuts-Off-Their-Heads stretched out his arm toward

her, and she took him by the hand. Then together they turned toward the road that would lead them out of the Suwali country and into the land of the Real People, and they ran.

Thirteen

THERE WAS a big celebration that night in Ijodi following the return of Edohi and his band of triumphant warriors. Most of the people from the neighboring town of Kituwah were also there, and everyone joined in the festivities. The women of Ijodi cooked lots of food, and everyone feasted heartily. Individual warriors boasted of their most recent exploits, and there was singing and dancing far into the night. Edohi danced and sang with the others, but he did not choose to boast of his exploits. Then at one point, following the end of a dance, his maternal uncle did it for him. Hemp Carrier walked to the center of the dancing circle to address the crowd. It was not difficult for him to get their attention, for the Real People loved to listen to a good speech, and Hemp Carrier was known to most of them as a fine orator. Anytime he spoke in public, his language was formal and precise, and his voice was sonorous, deep and mellow. They all gave Hemp Carrier their full attention.

"My brothers and sisters," he cried out, and then he lowered his voice to continue. "I am but a poor speaker, but I have some things I want to say to you."

A few people in the crowd chuckled quietly and gave one another knowing looks. Hemp Carrier always preceded his speeches with this same self-deprecating and erroneous statement.

"We have listened," he continued, "to the exploits of many of the fine warriors of the Real People who went to the land of the Suwalis and helped to destroy the village there, but we have not heard the best. We have not heard from my nephew, Edohi.

"It was Edohi who planned this raid, and it was Edohi who led it. Edohi was the first one to reach an enemy, the first one to kill. We've had a great victory there over our enemies, the Suwalis, because of Edohi.

"The Suwalis dared to insult us by attacking and destroying Taskigi, but things have now been balanced out between the Real People and the *Ani-Suwali.*

"When we attacked them, they screamed and ran in confusion and fright. And even so, we did not do as the Suwalis do, as they did at Taskigi and at other places we know of. We did not make war on women and children. Nor did we make war on the old or on the infirm. And this was at Edohi's insistence, at the insistence of our leader. We fought only their young men, their warriors, and we killed them all, all who were brave enough to stand and fight with us.

"Edohi led us to this victory, the same Edohi who led us before in the fight to free us, all of us, from the tyranny of the *Ani-Kutani* under which we all suffered for so long, and there we were successful as well. The *Ani-Kutani* are no more. Many of you here took part in that bloody battle. Many of you won honors there, and if you were there, you know that it was Edohi who brought it all about.

"I am his maternal uncle, my brothers and sisters, and so perhaps it is not my place to make such a proposal, but I think that we should make Edohi permanent chief of our town, chief of Ijodi. Because I'm his uncle, I will not speak of it again, but you can think about it and talk about it among yourselves, and if you think that I am wrong about this, then just don't do anything, and you won't hear any more about it from me, but if you think that I am right, then you can act on it for yourselves. All of you know, though, as well as I, that something has to be done soon about the condition of our town. You know what things have been like with us. And what more capable leader do we have among us than Edohi? I know of no such person.

"Edohi deserves a better spokesman than I, but I am his maternal uncle, and I had these few thoughts which I wanted to tell you. Now I will say no more."

Hemp Carrier sat down to loud cheering and praise, both for himself and for Edohi, and Edohi was suddenly overwhelmed by well-wishers and admirers, all wanting to congratulate him at once. Off to one side, Wild Hemp, his mother, stood beaming with pride. The Spoiler walked over to stand beside her.

"Your son has just received great praise," she said.

"Yes," said Wild Hemp.

"And it's all well deserved, I think," said the Spoiler. "Edohi is a fine young man. All of the men who went to the Suwali country this time did well. They all deserve our praise, but Edohi is especially deserving."

Wild Hemp made no response other than her continued beaming with nearly overweening pride.

"I think," said the Spoiler, "that your brother's idea is a good one. We need a chief over this town, and what better choice is there? I think there is no other. He showed his wisdom also by the way in which he settled the dispute between his clan and the Paint People and at the same time made my man into a Real Person. Yes. He's the right choice to be our chief."

"Do you really think so?" said Wild Hemp.

"Yes, I do, and I think that we should meet with our clan sisters to discuss it. You with yours and I with mine, and we should tell the women of the other clans to do the same. Look over there."

The Spoiler nodded in Edohi's direction, and Wild Hemp followed the nod. Edohi was there with Sohi. The two mothers smiled.

"If he's to be a chief," said the Spoiler, "it would be much better if he had a wife."

"Yes," said Wild Hemp. "It would. And it's time, I think."

Across the way, Groundhog's Brother and others from Kituwah were gathered in a small group talking. All of them had taken part in the battle with the Suwalis.

"Hemp Carrier made a good talk," said Groundhog's Brother. "This idea of a chief for the town seems like a good one to me. We should consider that for Kituwah. Maybe each town should do the same."

"Maybe so," said one of his companions, "but I don't know."

"When we are back home," said Groundhog's Brother, "let's talk to the women about this idea."

"You mean for us, in our town?"

"Yes. We'll talk to the women and see what they think about it."

"My mother is just over there," said one of the men from Kituwah. "I'll go right now and find out what she thinks about it."

Sohi was about to take her leave of Edohi, but as she turned to walk away, he reached out and put a hand on her shoulder.

"Wait," he said.

She stopped and turned back toward him. She was smaller than her sister had been, with more delicate features, and she had a milder disposition, quiet and somewhat demure.

"Yes?" she said.

"Sohi," he said. "I've been thinking. I think I've remained alone long enough now. Do you think I'm right about that?"

"Yes," she said. "It's been long enough, I think. Mother thinks so, too. I've heard her say it more than once."

"You have? I'm glad to hear that. Well then, if your mother agrees to it, and if old Gone-in-the-Water says that it will work out," said Edohi, "would you be willing to be my wife?"

"If my mother agrees, and if your mother agrees," said Sohi, "then, yes. I would be willing, and I'd be well pleased."

"I'll talk to my mother and my uncle," he said. "They'll arrange things with your people. You're very beautiful, Sohi. I'll tell my uncle and my mother to hurry things along as quickly as they can."

"I'll be waiting, Edohi," Sohi said, and to herself she said, I've been waiting for you to do this for a long time, a very long time. She smiled, and she turned and walked away. Edohi watched her until she had passed into the crowd beyond his sight. She would make a fine wife, he thought, but he was a little sad. He did not feel about her the way he had felt about her sister, and something deep inside told him that he could never feel that way again. Perhaps it was a thing of youth, that feeling. Perhaps it was a thing that could only happen once in one man's life. He didn't know. It was probably one of those great mysteries of life. And Edohi only knew that he had once had something and then lost it, and although the terrible anguish and nearly unbearable pain had passed with time, a dull aching sadness remained, and the thing that had been lost could never be regained.

Cuts-Off-Their-Heads and the Suwali woman Rising Fawn had finally made their way out of the Suwali country and into the land of the Real People, but they still had a long walk ahead of them before they would reach a town. Of course, Cuts-Off-Their-Heads's own town was gone, destroyed by the Suwalis, so they could not go there. They would have to go someplace else. Ijodi, he thought, would be the closest, the easiest for them to reach. He wondered if anyone else from Taskigi had survived the terrible Suwali attack. If they had, he reasoned, they would most likely have gone for shelter to Ijodi. So he would surely find out about them there.

Then it occurred to him that almost certainly there had been other survivors, and surely they had gone to Ijodi. They had probably told the tale of the slaughter there, and the warriors of Ijodi had organized the reprisal against the Suwalis. It had probably been a force from Ijodi that had burned the Suwali town. The more he thought about it, the more certain he felt that he now had it all figured out, just the way it had happened.

So he decided that they would go to Ijodi, he and his Suwali woman. There he would hear all the latest news, and he would confirm his speculation about what had happened.

They were walking on the road now, no longer afraid of any possible surprise attacks by Suwalis, and it was late at night. Even so, Cuts-Off-Their-Heads could see just ahead a clearing beside the otherwise tree-lined road. It looked to him like a comfortable spot for a camp. It was fairly level and not too rocky.

"Let's stop up there," he said. "We'll rest until daylight returns, and then we'll go on to Ijodi."

"What will your people do to me when we get there?" said Rising Fawn. "Will they kill me?"

"No," he said. "Of course not. You're my woman now. No one would dare do anything to my woman."

"They won't like me, though, because I'm Suwali," she said.

"Maybe. At first. But they'll get used to you, and they'll accept you. Sooner or later, they'll grow to like you. You'll see."

They had reached the clearing, and they walked off the road to select a spot to sit down on the ground. Cuts-Off-Their-Heads wished that he had taken the time to return to the cave that had given him temporary shelter outside of the Suwali village in order to retrieve his stolen blanket. But at that time he had to get away fast. He couldn't have taken the time, and he couldn't have been bothered with it anyway. The woman had still been trying to escape from him then. He looked at her, and he smiled. Her face was almost enchanting in the moonlight.

"Why did you decide to come with me?" he said.

"Aren't you glad that I did?"

"Yes. I am glad. But our people are enemies, and I stole you away. You hated me for that. You fought with me. You said that you would never willingly be mine. You even said that you'd kill me one day. I only wonder why you changed your mind."

She turned her face away from him and picked at some blades of grass there beside her. For a long time she was silent.

"I don't know," she said. "Maybe I'm crazy."

Then she laughed, and he laughed with her.

"Maybe you are," he said. "I think only a crazy woman would want to go with me."

She turned to him, suddenly serious, and she put a hand on his chest.

"Oh, no," she said. "You're handsome. I know. I've seen every bit of you. Remember? And you're brave, too. But you're also very kind. You never hit me, and you never tried to force yourself on me. Then finally you told me I could go back home. You said that I was free to go. It was then that I realized that I did not want you to be hurt or killed, and then I knew that I wanted to go on with you after all."

"Then that must have been when you knew that you were crazy," he said.

"Yes," she said, and laughing, she pulled him roughly to her. His arms went around her as she lay back in the grass, still pulling him to her, and gently he moved on top of her. His cheek brushed hers, and he was breathing heavily. He could scarcely believe this was happening to him.

"If you are crazy," he said, "then so am I, and I want to be crazy with you for the rest of my years."

Fourteen

"HE'S SO YOUNG," said Walnut.

"Yes," said Dancing Rabbit. "I know, and I knew as well that you would say that and feel that way. But what have I been able to do for the boy? I'm his maternal uncle, and I've done very little. Until just recently, I wasn't able to give him any of my time."

His sister knew what Dancing Rabbit meant by that. She knew that he was making reference to the years that he had spent in Men's Town as a priest, but she also knew that he did not want to discuss those years openly and out loud. His references to those times were always oblique.

"And now that I have the time," he continued, "I am not really fit to teach him the ways of a hunter or a warrior."

"What do you do with him when you go out of town and stay for so long?" Walnut asked.

"Oh, we just talk," said Dancing Rabbit. He did not like lying to his sister, but he couldn't confide even in her.

No one could know the secret of the writing. "I tell him the old tales. Sometimes we study plants. We talk about what is right and what is wrong.

"But my responsibility to him is for more than that. As his maternal uncle I should prepare him for the life of a man. I think I can do that by taking him with me on these trips I'm planning to make as a trader. He'll learn fast, and when he's grown, he'll have an occupation. He'll be ready to face life as a man."

"Well," said Walnut, "I suppose you're right. I'll miss him, but go ahead. I'll miss you both."

"*Wado*, sister," said Dancing Rabbit. "I'll take good care of him."

"I know you will."

"He'll learn fast and make us both proud of him. I'll go find him now and tell him."

Dancing Rabbit was more excited than ever to get started on his first trading venture now that he knew Gnat could go with him. Of course, he hadn't yet spoken to his nephew about it, but he was sure that the boy would want to join him on the expedition.

Then he thought again about Edohi and Edohi's plan to organize some kind of government for the Real People to bring an end to the chaos. Edohi wanted his help in working out the new system, and he had, however hesitantly, agreed. I was a fool, he said to himself. I should not have said what I did to him. It's too dangerous, and I have other things to do with my time. I have to think about my own safety and about the future of my nephew.

Besides, he thought, Edohi was already beginning to set things right. He had successfully brought to a conclusion the different clan feuds. He would do all right by himself. Dancing Rabbit realized that he was still afraid. He was still fearful that someone would decide after all to kill him because of his former life as a *Kutani*, and because of that fear, he wanted to get away from his own people just as soon as he could.

In a short time he found his nephew, and the two of them found a spot beside the stream where it ran through the town where they could sit and talk alone and undisturbed. They sat on the ground with their feet in the water, and the water was cool and pleasant.

"Nephew," said Dancing Rabbit, "I've decided to be-come a trader."

"A trader?"

"That's right. I'll take things of ours, things that are made by the Real People and things that we have in our country, and I'll carry them away to other people who don't have those things. There I'll trade for things that we don't have in our country and for things they make that are different from our own."

"Where will you go?"

"I'll go south, I think, at least for the first trip."

"But the *Ani-Chahta* and the *Ani-Cusa* live south of us. And other enemies of the Real People."

"I think I'll be safe," said Dancing Rabbit. "The people around us here, even our enemies, know how to behave properly. They don't often bother a trader, because the trader brings things to everyone."

Gnat stared into the water, watching it race over his own feet and on to wherever it was going. He wondered where it went.

"Will you be gone for a long time?" he asked.

"It will be a long trip," said his uncle. "I don't know just how long it will take. Not as long as that other trip I took."

"The one to the West?"

"Yes. Not so long as that one. But, Nephew?"

"Yes?"

"I want you to go with me on this trading trip."

Gnat turned to face Dancing Rabbit and sat up on his knees in his excitement.

"Really? You want me to go?"

"Yes," said Dancing Rabbit. "I said so."

Gnat sank back down to the ground, and a gloomy look came over his face.

"Mother won't let me go," he said.

"Of course she will."

"You think so?"

"I know that your mother will let you go with me," said Dancing Rabbit. "I know it, because I've already talked to her about it, and she told me that you could go with me."

"She did?"

"Yes. She did. Now do you really want to go? It will be a long trip. You'll be away from home, from your friends and from your mother."

"But I'll be with you."

"Even though what I said about traders is true, most people let them pass unharmed, there will still be dangers."

"I'm not afraid."

Dancing Rabbit smiled. He was proud of this son of his sister.

"Then we'll go," he said. "You and I."

"How soon, Uncle?" asked Gnat.

"I don't know. Maybe in the morning. Maybe the next day."

Again Gnat's enthusiasm gave way to disappointment. Dancing Rabbit saw the long face.

"What's wrong?" he said. "Is that too soon for you?"

"You told Edohi that you'd help him with what he's trying to do," said Gnat.

"Yes, I did. But Edohi doesn't need me."

"Have you told Edohi that you're going on a trip?"

"No."

Gnat stood up and turned his back to his uncle. He shuffled his wet feet back into his moccasins.

"I think I'll stay here," he said.

"Why?" asked Dancing Rabbit. "Because of Edohi?"

Gnat stood silent.

"Is that the reason you don't want to go with me?"

"Yes," said Gnat, and he turned around almost fiercely to face his uncle again. "You said you'd help him. He's counting on you."

Dancing Rabbit fell on his back and folded his arms over his chest. His feet still in the water, he looked up at the clouds that slowly passed by overhead. One of them, he thought, looked very like a rabbit.

"All right," he said. "Don't pout at me. I'll wait until Edohi says he doesn't need me here, and then we'll go. All right?"

"All right," said Gnat.

"Then you can walk with me over to Ijodi to see him, and we'll go right now."

· · · ·

People began to shout as soon as Cuts-Off-Their-Heads and his Suwali woman arrived at Ijodi. The people from Taskigi were surprised and happy to see him alive. Since he had not been with them when they escaped and fled to Ijodi, they had assumed he had been killed by the Suwalis.

"Look," they shouted. "Look who's here. Look who's alive."

Soon a crowd had gathered around him. They shouted questions at him, but he couldn't answer them, because they kept asking more questions. At last they quieted down some, and he spoke to them.

"I was knocked unconscious during the fight," he said, "and the Suwalis carried me away with them. They took me to one of their towns and tied me to a pole, but I escaped in the night."

"Did you kill any of them?" asked one.

"No. I slipped away in the night."

"But you stole a woman," said another with glee.

A woman reached out to strike the Suwali woman, and Cuts-Off-Their-Heads grabbed her by the wrist to prevent the blow.

"This is not a captive," he said. "This woman came with me by her own choice. I told her I wanted her, and she came."

"A Suwali woman," said a woman from Taskigi. "Ha."

"She's my woman, and I'm her man, and anyone who mistreats her will have to answer to me," said Cuts-Off-Their-Heads. "And her name is Rising Fawn. She cannot yet speak our language, but she speaks the trade language well."

But no one would call the Suwali woman by her name.

They called her instead, in their own language, Agehyuh Suwali, Suwali Woman, and that became her name.

At the suggestion of Edohi, Wild Hemp used her influence with her clan, the Bird People, to find a place in Ijodi for Suwali Woman to build her house, and in a few more days, the Bird People adopted Suwali Woman into their clan. Like the Shawnee, Suwali Woman had become a Real Person.

But she had not been forgotten back at her home. Her brother, who was called Snake, was determined to find her and bring her home. At first the Suwalis had fallen for Cuts-Off-Their-Heads's ruse. They had followed his tracks until they led into the water, and then they had lost him. Thinking that he was trying to return to his own home, they had gone on awhile in the direction of the Real People's country, but at last they had given up and gone back home.

Their captive had escaped them. But then a few days later Rising Fawn had disappeared. When they realized that she was indeed gone, they had searched the area, and someone had located the cave in which Cuts-Off-Their-Heads had been living. They had surmised that someone, perhaps the escaped captive, had been hiding there and had stolen the young woman away. After several days of searching for tracks, they had finally given up. All except Snake.

Snake armed himself with a knife, a warclub, a bow and some arrows. He took an extra pair of moccasins, some dried corn and some dried venison, and he headed for the land of the Real People. He couldn't be sure, of course, but he thought that the escaped captive had stolen his sister. He wanted her back. He did not know what the Real People would do with a captive woman of the Suwalis, but he did not think that it would be pleasant. He hoped that he could locate her and rescue her before it was too late, before they killed her. They might not kill her, of course. One of their men, perhaps the very one who stole her away, might make her his wife, whether she wanted him or not. If that happened, she would be little better than a slave.

It was almost midday, and he had thought about stopping at the border town which was just ahead for something to eat. Then he saw it. There was nothing but ashes. He was astonished at the devastation. There was no smoke, so he knew that the ashes were cold and the ones who had done the deed were long gone.

He rushed into the town and looked around. He saw no bodies. He saw nothing but the ashes of what had been the homes of his friends and relatives. He dropped to his knees and dug his hands down into the ashes. He knew at once who had done this. It had to be the Mountain People, the old enemies of the Suwalis, the people of the very man he was pursuing. He looked up to the sky and let out a long, loud wail which was at once a cry of mourning and a cry of hatred. Then he heard a sound behind him, and he pulled the knife out of its sheath and whirled. There stood a wretched-looking Suwali man.

"Snake," said the man, "is that you?"

"Yes. And you? I should know you, I think."

"I'm Water Traveler."

"Yes. Of course. Who did this to your town?"

"It was our old enemies the Mountain People," said Water Traveler. "They came on us by surprise. We should have been ready for them. We should have expected them. We burned one of their towns not long ago."

"Yes. I know. Are you— Are you the only one left?"

"No. There are a few others. Mostly women and children. Most of the men stayed to fight."

"Where have you been?" asked Snake. "These ashes are cold. Why didn't you come to—"

"We waited here," Water Traveler said, interrupting Snake. "We hid in the woods waiting for the Mountain People to leave. We didn't want to leave our dead unattended. We waited until we thought it was safe. Then we came back to take care of the bodies. We were just about ready to go up to your town when I saw you here. Now you can go back with us."

"No," said Snake. "You and the others go on and tell them what happened here. I have something else to do."

So the Mountain People had retaliated, and they had hit hard. In the mind of Snake, that new information made the fate of his sister even more uncertain, and it made his mission even more urgent. He would have to hurry, and he would have to be careful. It would do no good to get himself killed or captured. His sister was in danger.

Snake wanted her back. He walked the trail as long as he was in his own country, but when he had gone beyond the territory in which he felt safe, he took to the woods. He did not want to get into a fight with his enemies if he could avoid it. An unplanned battle would not help the chances of his mission, and his mission was the important thing. He was not looking for war honors or prizes, and he was not looking for revenge. He was going to find his sister and bring her safely back home.

Now and then Snake went back to the road to check for tracks, hoping to find something he could recognize. At last he was successful. He thought that he was deep in enemy territory, but he wasn't sure. He had not been far in that direction before. He had not been a part of the band that had gone to attack Taskigi. But he had gone a great distance from his home, and the road was leading him somewhere.

He found a place beside the road where someone had camped for the night recently, and he studied the campsite carefully. Most of the sign was not clear, but he found one moccasin print that he could read, and he was sure that it belonged to Rising Fawn. He continued his journey, again moving through the woods but following the road.

Then he found himself climbing a steep hill. The combination of the difficulty of the climb and the thickness of the woods with its tangled undergrowth made him feel particularly vulnerable, so he moved even more slowly than the climb necessitated. He stopped now and then to look around, to be sure that he was not being observed by some enemy. Then finally he came to the top of the hill.

It was broad and clear, almost flat. He studied it awhile before venturing out in the open. Then he walked across to the other side, and he found himself looking down on the road and on a town. It was a walled town, and it seemed to be populous and busy. From his vantage point up above, he could see over the walls and could see the people moving around in there, but he was too far away to be able to recognize anyone in there. But it was the first town he had come to in the enemy country. He had a strong feeling that somewhere down there in that town, he would find his sister.

Fifteen

AND SO THERE WAS another consultation with Gone-in-the-Water by the Spoiler, and there was another favorable prediction. And following that, there was another wedding for Edohi. But all could tell, even the bride, that Edohi's enthusiasm was not what it had been the first time. Sohi would have liked for her husband to be more enthusiastic, but she understood his feelings. She knew, at least she thought that she knew, how deep was the love between her lost sister and Edohi. And she knew that she could never expect to receive from him that same level of devotion, the same intensity of passion. She did not look for it. Yet inside she longed for it.

It happened with the Suwali woman just as it had happened with the Shawnee. Many people gave her hard looks and refused to speak to her. Some spoke or nodded in a cursory manner, and a very few talked with her as new neighbors and friends. The most friendly, of course, were the Bird People, for Suwali Woman, as they had come to call her, had become a Bird Person by adoption. It was as if she had been born to them. And Cuts-Off-Their-Heads was very happy. Life would have seemed perfect to him were it not for the remaining hostility toward his wife. On several occasions he very nearly got into a fight on that account. But Edohi was watching, aware that a new volatile situation existed in his town. He did not want anything to renew the old clan feuds of the recent past.

Edohi would have liked to have more free time to spend with his own new wife, but he had the business of the government of the town to worry about and this more recent problem with Suwali Woman.

And still up on the mountain outside of Ijodi, the Suwali Snake kept watch. He had watched several of the people from the town below walk out alone, and he could have killed any of them, but that was not the reason he had come. He had come to rescue his sister and to kill the man who had abducted her. Nothing more and nothing less. And he would do nothing to diminish his chances of accomplishing that goal. So he waited and he watched.

He kept quiet and well hidden up on the mountaintop overlooking Ijodi. He slept little and ate even less. He had used up his trail food, and there was little to be gathered on top of the mountain. But he had fasted before, and he knew that he could go for days without food and still have his strength. He did not know how long he would have to wait, but he had resolved that he would not go home without his sister. He would do what he came to do, or he would die in the attempt.

. . . .

Dancing Rabbit stood and looked over the pile of goods he had accumulated for his trading venture, and he heaved a heavy sigh. The trip would have to wait. He was standing in his sister's house. She was there preparing a stew. Across the room, Gnat lounged on the cot against the wall. It was early morning, and they had just returned from their ritual morning dip in the river. Dancing Rabbit turned to face his nephew.

"I'm going to Ijodi," he said. "Do you want to walk with me?"

"Yes," said Gnat. "May I go, Mother?"

"Of course. But you should eat something first, both of you."

Soon their bellies were full, and they were on their way. They walked for a while in silence.

"Are you going to see Edohi?" Gnat asked.

"Yes."

"What will you do?"

"I don't know," said Dancing Rabbit. "We'll talk."

"Will you talk about the government?"

"We don't have any government," said Dancing Rabbit. "We'll talk about the need for one."

"It's dangerous for you," said Gnat. "Isn't it?"

"It might be. Because I was a *Kutani*. If I talk with Edohi about government, some might think that I'll be trying to re-establish the *Ani-Kutani*."

"But that's not what you'll be doing, is it?"

"No. It's not. But we do have to have something."

They walked farther, again in silence.

"Uncle?" said Gnat.

"Yes, Nephew?"

"I shouldn't have talked you into staying. We could go on the trip to the south to trade. Maybe by the time we get back, Edohi will have everything taken care of. Maybe it will be safe for you when we get back."

"And maybe not," said Dancing Rabbit. "No, Nephew. You were right. I was trying to avoid my responsibility. You set me straight again. This business must be resolved before we go."

They were close to Ijodi, already in the shadow of the big mountain there. Gnat looked up and saw a figure there on the ridge.

"Look, Uncle," he said. "Someone's up there watching over the town."

Dancing Rabbit looked, and he, too, saw the figure there. It was just about at the flat rocks where he knew that Edohi used to muse long hours.

"It must be Edohi," he said. "Come on. We'll join him up there. That will be better than going into Ijodi anyway."

Dancing Rabbit led the way, and his nephew followed. They left the road and found the path which led up the mountainside. At first the climb was easy, but it grew steeper as they neared the top. The last short distance, they had to climb with hands and feet, but there were plenty of large rocks there to provide both handholds and steps. When they found themselves on top of the mountain, they were winded. They stood for a moment, taking deep breaths and looking around.

"Where is Edohi?" said Gnat.

Dancing Rabbit gestured with his chin toward the flat rock. It was off to their left.

"He was right there," he said.

"Maybe he doesn't want to see us."

"Maybe," said Dancing Rabbit, "but I don't think so. Probably he just didn't see us coming. He should be around somewhere. Come on. Let's look around."

They walked toward the flat rock, and as they went, they looked in all directions. There was no sign of Edohi or of anyone else.

"He was up here," said Gnat.

"Yes," said Dancing Rabbit. "I saw him, too."

At the rock he stopped, and he turned to look again all around. Then he stepped up on the rock and looked down on the town.

"He must be up here," he said. "If he had gone down another way, we could see him from up here. He wouldn't be in the town yet."

He turned back around and jumped down off the rock.

"Let's look over that way," he said.

He started walking away from the rock, and Gnat turned to follow. Just then the Suwali Snake jumped out from behind the rock. He wrapped his left arm around Gnat's neck and placed the tip of a flint knife just under the boy's right ear.

"Uncle," said Gnat.

Dancing Rabbit turned, and his eyes opened wide. He spread his arms and bent his knees, crouched for action.

"Do you talk the trade talk?" said Snake.

"Yes," said Dancing Rabbit. "What do you want with us?"

"I don't want to harm this boy. I want a man to kill."

"Let him go then," said Dancing Rabbit, "and kill me."

"I don't want to kill you either. I want a man down there."

He nodded his head toward Ijodi.

"Tell me," said Dancing Rabbit.

"I am of the Suwali. My name is Snake. Some of my people captured this man from the town they burned. He escaped from us, and he took my sister with him. I followed them here. I came to kill him and to take my sister back home."

"I know nothing about all that," said Dancing Rabbit. "What is the man's name?"

"I don't know his name, but if you find him and my sister and bring them to me, I'll let this boy go unharmed."

There seemed to be no options. If Dancing Rabbit tried anything, the man would be able to kill Gnat almost immediately. Even if Dancing Rabbit were able to defeat him, it would be too late for Gnat.

"Nephew," he said, "don't be afraid. I'll go down and find the man he wants."

"And my sister," said Snake.

"Yes," said Dancing Rabbit. "The man and the woman."

"I'm not afraid, Uncle," said Gnat.

"Wait," said Snake.

"Yes?"

"Find the man. Tell him to come up here with my sister. You stay below. If anyone besides the man and my sister comes up here, I'll kill this boy. If you do as I ask, I'll let this boy go as soon as they arrive."

"No one will come but those you ask for," said Dancing Rabbit, and he turned and headed down the hill.

In Ijodi, Dancing Rabbit found Edohi.

"I'm glad you're here," said Edohi. "We have much to discuss."

"Not yet," said Dancing Rabbit. "Do you have a man here who stole a Suwali woman?"

"Yes," said Edohi. "Cuts-Off-Their-Heads came home with a Suwali woman. She's his wife now. They live here."

"Will you take me to see them?"

Edohi led the way to Suwali Woman's new house, and Dancing Rabbit was relieved to find that they were both at home. Edohi made the introductions.

"Sit down," said Suwali Woman, and she spoke in the language of the Real People. She was already using a few words and phrases, and she was obviously proud of her accomplishment.

"I don't have time to sit," said Dancing Rabbit. "My nephew's life is in danger."

"How can we help?" said Cuts-Off-Their-Heads.

"It involves you," said Dancing Rabbit. "We were coming here to see Edohi. Just outside of town we saw a man on the mountain. He was sitting there on the flat rock. We thought it was Edohi, and so we climbed the mountain. But it was not Edohi. It was a Suwali man. He called himself Snake."

"My brother," said Suwali Woman.

"Yes," said Dancing Rabbit. "He said so. He said he came here to take you home and to kill the man who stole you away. He has my nephew up there. If you fail to go up to him, he'll kill my nephew."

"Let's go then," said Cuts-Off-Their-Heads.

"Wait," said Dancing Rabbit. "Take your weapons. He means to fight with you and kill you. And you two alone must go. He said if more came, he'd kill my nephew. We have to keep this knowledge to ourselves."

"What will we do?" Suwali Woman asked her husband, reverting to the trade language.

"We have to go," he said. "We can't let him kill this boy."

"But he'll kill you," she said, "or you'll kill him. I don't want either one of you to be killed."

"When we get up there," said Cuts-Off-Their-Heads, "you tell him that, just as soon as the boy is safe. Maybe no one will be killed. Now come on."

"Do you know the path up the mountainside?" asked Edohi.

"No," said Cuts-Off-Their-Heads, "but we can find our way."

"No," said Dancing Rabbit. "I'll take you as far as the path at the bottom of the mountain, and I'll wait there for my nephew to come down. And I'll wait there for you, too."

"I'll go and wait with you," said Edohi.

Edohi and Dancing Rabbit stood at the bottom of the mountain path and watched while Cuts-Off-Their-Heads and Suwali Woman started up. They watched the two until they lost sight of them, and then they watched the path, waiting for something to happen. It seemed a long wait. Both men had climbed this same path, Edohi many times, and it seemed to them both that they could climb up there in much less time than the time they stood there waiting. Then they saw a form up above. It was someone coming down. They strained their eyes until they could recognize the form.

"It's Gnat," said Dancing Rabbit.

"Yes," said Edohi.

Still they stayed at the bottom. They had said that they would. They waited until Gnat made his way down to join them.

"Did he harm you?" said Dancing Rabbit.

"No, Uncle," said Gnat. "I'm all right. But I think that they're going to fight."

"Yes," said Dancing Rabbit. "That's what the Suwali man came for. To fight and to kill the man who carried off his sister."

"Can't we go back up and help?" said Gnat.

"No," said Dancing Rabbit. "I promised that I'd do as he asked if he would let you go unharmed. He's done that, and we have to do what we said. We can't interfere."

Sixteen

I T WAS SUWALI WOMAN who first appeared on top of the mountain. When Snake saw her, he shouted out her name in their own language.

"Rising Fawn," he said. "Are you all right?"

"Yes," she said, also speaking Suwali. "I'm just fine. Brother, you shouldn't have come here. It's dangerous for you. You're surrounded by your enemies."

"I'm not afraid," said Snake.

Just then Cuts-Off-Their-Heads made his appearance from over the edge. He stepped up bravely and looked directly, threateningly, at the Suwali. He heard the conversation that was taking place between his wife and her brother, but he could not understand the words.

"Is this the man that stole you away from us?" Snake asked his sister.

"Yes," she said, "but—"

"Wait," said Snake. "First I must let this boy go free."

Snake released Gnat, and Gnat stood for a moment, confused.

"Go on," said Snake.

Gnat stood still.

Suwali Woman turned to her husband and spoke in the trade language.

"He's telling the boy to go," she said.

"Go on down," said Cuts-Off-Their-Heads, speaking in the language of the Real People. "Your uncle is waiting for you down below with Edohi."

Gnat walked to the path. He stopped and looked around once more. Then he started down. The three left on top of the mountain stood for a moment in tense silence. Then Snake spoke to his sister in their own Suwali tongue.

"I came to take you home," he said, "and to kill the man who stole you."

"He speaks the trade language," said Suwali Woman. "Let's use that. And he's your brother-in-law. His name is Cuts-Off-Their-Heads."

"I came here to kill you, Cuts-Off-Their-Heads."

"I'm not afraid to fight you," said Cuts-Off-Their-Heads, "but I don't want to fight you. Your sister is my wife."

"You stole her."

"Yes. I did."

"He stole me," said Suwali Woman, "but he didn't harm me, and later he let me go. I came with him after that of my own choice. I came with him because I wanted to be his wife."

"I swore to fight this man," said Snake, "and to take you home with me or to die here."

"There's no need for fighting," said Suwali Woman.

"I don't want to fight with you," said Cuts-Off-Their-Heads.

"Fight or die," said Snake, and he raised his warclub over his head and ran at Cuts-Off-Their-Heads. Cuts-Off-Their-Heads ducked to one side as Snake swung his club and dashed by. Both men turned to face each other. Snake stepped in and swung again, and Cuts-Off-Their-Heads grabbed Snake's wrist with both his hands. Snake's left hand reached for Cuts-Off-Their-Heads's face and clawed at his eyes, and with a roar, Cuts-Off-Their-Heads twisted Snake's arm, throwing the Suwali over on his back and causing him to drop his warclub. Cuts-Off-Their-Heads picked up the warclub and flung it over the side of the mountain. Snake was back on his feet. He drew the flint knife out and held it ready. Unarmed but braced for the attack, Cuts-Off-Their-Heads waited for the other to charge.

Snake rushed at him and stabbed out. Cuts-Off-Their-Heads jumped to the side, but the flint blade sliced him below his ribs.

"Ah," Cuts-Off-Their-Heads yelled in pain and anger. He spun on his left foot, kicking out with his right leg, and he caught the Suwali across the midsection, knocking the wind out of him. Snake doubled over, and Cuts-Off-Their-Heads rushed in, shoving him to the ground and wrenching the knife out of his fist. He rolled Snake over on his back and sat on his chest, holding the tip of the knife blade to Snake's throat. Snake was still gasping for breath.

Suwali Woman watched in fascinated horror. She was sure that her husband was about to slash the throat of her brother, and she knew that there was nothing she could do. Snake at last caught his breath.

"Go ahead," he said. "Kill me."

"No," said Cuts-Off-Their-Heads. "I won't kill my brother-in-law, but you are my prisoner. Get up. We're going down the mountain."

Snake said nothing. He did not resist further. He stood up and walked to the path, where he was the first of the three to descend. Cuts-Off-Their-Heads followed him, and Suwali Woman went last. When they got to the bottom, they found Edohi, Dancing Rabbit and Gnat waiting there for them.

"This is your wife's brother?" asked Edohi.

"Yes," said Cuts-Off-Their-Heads, "and he's my prisoner. We fought."

"What will you do with your prisoner?"

"I don't know," said Cuts-Off-Their-Heads. "He made me fight with him. I had to either kill him or capture him. There was no other way, unless he killed me."

"Let's go back into town," said Edohi. "Maybe we'll think of something. Of course, the decision will be yours to make."

Snake suffered jeers and a few blows on the way through the streets of Ijodi, but everyone respected the rights of the captor, so he wasn't harmed, was never even seriously threatened. At last they stopped in front of a house.

"This is your sister's house," said Cuts-Off-Their-Heads.

"My sister's house?" said Snake.

"Of course," said Cuts-Off-Their-Heads. "Women

own the houses among the Real People. Don't your women own their houses?"

"But my sister is not one of your people. She's a Suwali. She's one of your enemies."

"She's a Real Person now, adopted by the Bird People, and she's my wife. This is her house."

Snake stood silent for a moment as if in deep thought. Then he turned toward his sister.

"You came here of your own free will?" he asked.

"Yes," she said.

"Are you happy here living with this man?"

"Yes. I won't leave him. I mean to stay here with him until I die."

Snake turned back toward Cuts-Off-Their-Heads.

"What will you do with me now?" he said.

"If I leave you free to walk about," said Cuts-Off-Their-Heads, "will you promise me that you won't try to escape? You won't try to kill me or any of my people, and you won't try to take your sister back to your home?"

"My sister doesn't want to go back home," said Snake. "I'm your prisoner. I won't try to escape or kill you or any of your people, and I won't take my sister back against her will."

"Then you'll be as a guest in my wife's house," said Cuts-Off-Their-Heads, with a glance toward Suwali Woman, "if that's all right with her."

"Of course it is," said Suwali Woman. "Sit down and wait here, both of you, and I'll get you some food."

"That sounds good," said Snake. "I haven't eaten anything for several days."

Suwali Woman set about preparing the food, and the two men sat down in front of the house.

"Our people are enemies," said Cuts-Off-Their-Heads, "but your sister is my wife. Let's be friends."

"Your people burned one of our towns and killed the people there," said Snake.

"But only after your people burned one of our towns, the town where I lived. It was called Taskigi. They killed everyone there, men, women, children, all but those few who escaped. And me. They carried me away captive. A town for a town. Things are balanced once again between our two peoples."

"Yes," said Snake. "I suppose you're right. But you're my enemy."

Cuts-Off-Their-Heads rubbed his chin with his hand and stared at the dirt between his feet.

"I'm your brother-in-law," he said.

"I hear they're talking about making you war chief of Ijodi," said Dancing Rabbit.

"Yes," said Edohi. "There's been such talk."

"Will you accept the role?"

"I suppose," said Edohi. "Some kind of authority is needed, but there's something that's troubling me."

"What is it?" said Dancing Rabbit.

"I talked to Gone-in-the-Water a time ago. He said that everything comes in twos. Day and night. Light and dark. Summer and winter. Male and female. Everything."

"War and peace," said Dancing Rabbit.

"Yes."

"Then if you become war chief," said Dancing Rabbit, "someone else must be peace chief. Is that it?"

Edohi gave Dancing Rabbit a quick and astonished look. It was a sudden revelation from a former *Kutani*, and

Edohi knew right then that he had been right in seeking the help of Dancing Rabbit. Once expressed, it was such a simple idea. It seemed so obvious, so natural and so right.

"Yes," he said. "That is it. That's just what we need. A war chief and a peace chief. That's the beginning."

"Only the beginning?"

"Yes. Even with a war chief and a peace chief in each town, that's still too much power in only two men. The problem with the *Ani-Kutani* was that a few men had too much power."

"One man had all the power," said Dancing Rabbit.

"We can never let that happen again. The power must be with all the people."

"Then let each chief have a council of seven, one from each of the clans."

"Yes," said Edohi, "selected by the women of the clans, and the women should have the power to remove a man from the council if they don't approve of his actions."

"It's a good beginning," said Dancing Rabbit. "What do we do next?"

"We'll have to call a meeting of the whole town to propose this new way," said Edohi. "I'll talk to my mother and my uncle. They'll take care of calling the meeting. While we wait, let's think further about the new way. There are still lots of details to be worked out."

"All right," said Dancing Rabbit. "I agree. When will we meet again?"

"In four days, I think. I'll go to Kituwah then to see you."

"Good," said Dancing Rabbit. "But now, what will you do about the Suwali?"

"I don't know," said Edohi. "Cuts-Off-Their-Heads

144 · ROBERT J. CONLEY

won't want to kill his brother-in-law, I think. But many of
the people here will want to see him killed. It's a problem."

"The war chief," said Dancing Rabbit, "should probably be the man to deal with other peoples in any way, not
just in war. Perhaps you could use this man to bring an
end to our longtime war with the *Ani-Suwali*."

"I'll have to ask Cuts-Off-Their-Heads," said Edohi.
"The man is his prisoner. But it's a good thought. I'll see
about it. Thank you, my friend."

"I hope it works," said Dancing Rabbit. "And now I
think it's time for me to find my nephew and start back to
Kituwah. It will be late by the time we get there."

"In four days I'll see you there," said Edohi.

Dancing Rabbit left, and Edohi walked back to the house
of Suwali Woman. He found the captive, Snake, and
Cuts-Off-Their-Heads sitting in front of the house eating.

" '*Siyo*, Edohi," said Cuts-Off-Their-Heads. "Come
and eat with us."

"*Wado*," said Edohi, and he sat down there in front of
the house. Suwali Woman dished some stew into a bowl
and handed it to him with a carved wooden spoon. He
tasted it and smacked his lips.

"It's good," he said. "Thank you."

Suwali Woman beamed with pride. She dished some
out for herself and sat down to eat. No one spoke any
more until the bowls were empty. Then Edohi spoke to
Cuts-Off-Their-Heads, and he spoke in the language of
the Real People so that Snake could not understand.

"What will you do with your brother-in-law?" he asked.

"I don't know," said Cuts-Off-Their-Heads.

"Are you willing to set him free?"

"Yes. Of course. But what will the others say?"

"They will say nothing," said Edohi, "if I go with you and your wife back to the land of the Suwalis with him. We'll use him and your wife to get us in and out safely and to get the Suwali leaders to talk with us. I think that we can end the war with the Suwalis in this way. What do you think?"

"I don't know," said Cuts-Off-Their-Heads. "It might work. Let me ask my wife."

Cuts-Off-Their-Heads talked to Suwali Woman in the trade language. Both Snake and Edohi could understand, but neither of them interrupted the conversation between the man and his wife. At last Suwali Woman answered.

"I think it will work," she said. She looked at her brother. "What do you think?"

"It might work," he said.

"Are you willing to cooperate with us on this peace?" asked Edohi.

"This man could have killed me today," said Snake, "and he didn't. He's my brother-in-law now, and my sister has become one of your people. Yes. I'll help you to get this peace between our people."

Seventeen

EDOHI TALKED to his mother and his uncle about
the meeting of the whole town, and when the
fourth day had arrived he met with Dancing Rabbit at
Kituwah. Then on the seventh day he left for the Suwali
country in the company of Cuts-Off-Their-Heads, Suwali
Woman and Snake. All their conversation was in the trade
language, and the journey was uneventful until they
reached the Suwali country. Then in spite of his company
and his mission, Edohi became anxious. It was entirely
possible, he knew, that the Suwalis would kill him and
Cuts-Off-Their-Heads, that they would not listen to any
talk, not from him, not even from Suwali Woman and
Snake.

And what about Snake? Was he feigning friendship until he could get Edohi and Cuts-Off-Their-Heads at the
mercy of his own people? More deceitful things than that
had happened. And Snake was hard to figure out. He had
traveled to the country of the Real People to kill the man

who had carried off his sister. And even when he had discovered that she had gone willingly and that she was happy living as the wife of Cuts-Off-Their-Heads, he had fought with Cuts-Off-Their-Heads and tried to kill him. When Cuts-Off-Their-Heads had defeated him, Snake had become silent, taciturn and docile. He had been entirely cooperative, but he had not been really friendly. His heart did not seem to be in this mission. He seemed to be cooperating only because there was nothing else he could do.

Edohi waited for an opportunity to speak with Cuts-Off-Their-Heads alone. They stopped for a rest beside a cold, clear running stream, and when Suwali Woman and her brother went to the stream, Edohi held Cuts-Off-Their-Heads back, and he spoke to him in a low voice in the language of the Real People.

"We're in their country now," he said. "We've come on a mission of peace, and we know your wife's mind, but we don't know the mind of your brother-in-law, and we don't know what to expect from the other Suwalis. Be cautious."

"Yes," said Cuts-Off-Their-Heads. "I've been thinking the same thing."

"The meeting will take place four days after Edohi returns from the Suwali country," said Hemp Carrier. "Everyone in Ijodi has been informed."

"Did my son tell you what it is that he'll propose at this meeting?" asked Wild Hemp.

"No," said Hemp Carrier. "He only said that it will be about restoring order to the town. He called it a new way."

148 · ROBERT J. CONLEY

"Maybe he's going to be chief after all, as you suggested. I've heard people talking about it. I think everyone will agree."

"I don't think Edohi will agree," said Hemp Carrier. "He said to me that we killed the priests because they had too much power. He said that no one man should have so much power. Never again."

"But he would only be chief over Ijodi," said Wild Hemp. "Not over all the towns of the Real People. It wouldn't be the same as it was with the *Ani-Kutani.*"

"I said that to him, but he still said the same thing back. It would be too much power for one man."

"So what do you think he's going to say at this meeting?"

"I don't know."

Wild Hemp made a few more stitches on the moccasin she had been working on. Then she laid it aside.

"Let's go see Gone-in-the-Water," she said.

The old man was tying up some plants to the framework of the lean-to which was attached to the front of his house.

"That's good," he said. "They'll be dry enough in a few days. What's that? What did you say, Noisy?"

He looked around for a moment.

"Oh," he said. "Someone's coming? Well, let's get ready for them."

He took a seat there under his arbor to wait.

"No mischief now," he said. "We're going to have guests."

Soon he saw them, Wild Hemp and her brother Hemp Carrier. He filled the bowl of his pipe with tobacco from his pouch, stood up again and shuffled over to the small fire which burned there before his house. He picked up a burning faggot and lit the tobacco, then returned to his seat. By then his visitors had arrived.

" *'Siyo,* " he said. "Come and sit down with me."

They chatted for a while about the weather and other things, before Hemp Carrier decided to bring up the subject of their visit.

"Uncle," he said, using the polite form of address, "we've called a town meeting to take place four days after the return of Edohi from the Suwali country."

"Yes," said Gone-in-the-Water. "I know about it."

"You know everything," said Hemp Carrier. "That's the reason we've come to visit with you. It was my nephew, Edohi, who asked for this meeting. I suggested earlier that Edohi should be chief of Ijodi, but Edohi doesn't think that would be right."

"Edohi's a wise man, for such a young man," said the conjurer.

"But if he's not going to be chief, then why does he want this meeting?" Hemp Carrier asked.

The old man puffed on his pipe until his face was clouded to the view of his visitors. Hemp Carrier could not be sure, but he thought that the old man appeared to have cocked his head slightly to one side, as if he were listening carefully to what someone was saying. And then he thought that the old head nodded slowly, as if in agreement. Then Gone-in-the-Water spoke through the cloud.

"Everything we know exists in pairs," he said. "Day and night. Light and dark. Summer and winter. Male and female."

"Edohi said that to me," said Wild Hemp.

"Yes," said Gone-in-the-Water. "He would. And war and peace."

"But what has that to do with our meeting?" asked Hemp Carrier.

"It's something for you to consider," said the old man.

"Edohi has been talking to Dancing Rabbit, the man who was once a *Kutani*," said Hemp Carrier.

"That's wise. The *Kutani* will remember the old ways and help combine them with the new."

"So what should we do while we're waiting for Edohi to return? How should we prepare for this meeting?" asked Wild Hemp.

"The meeting will work out as it should," said the conjurer, "but if you feel a need to prepare, go to Kituwah and talk with the *Kutani*. He'll tell you what he and Edohi have planned together. Then you can talk to others while you're waiting, and maybe the meeting will go smoother and faster. That's all."

Brother and sister thanked the old man and left, not at all sure that they had accomplished anything by their visit. Gone-in-the-Water watched them go, and when they disappeared from his view, he had smoked up the tobacco in his pipe. He laid it aside and went back to his work. He tied up two more plants and stepped back to study the results of his labors.

"Eh?" he said. "What was that? Oh, yes. You're right. I do need some *atali-guli*, some of that mountain climber, the little person. Let's go get it then. Come along."

"How much farther is your town?" Edohi asked, speaking the trade language.

"Not far," said Snake.

Edohi knew that just ahead was the charred site of the village he had attacked and burned. He had noticed that the two Suwalis had grown silent and tense. He and Cuts-Off-Their-Heads had too. The killing that had taken place up ahead was recent, fresh in all their minds. He had only asked the question to break the heavy, uncomfortable silence that had fallen over them.

Just then seven Suwali warriors stepped out of the woods to block the path. They were painted and heavily armed, and their faces wore surly looks. Edohi and his companions stopped. A tense moment of silence followed before Snake stepped forward and spoke in his own tongue to the warriors. One man among them stepped forward to greet Snake, and a brief conversation followed. Then, suddenly, the Suwalis rushed forward and swarmed on Edohi and Cuts-Off-Their-Heads. The struggles of the two Real People were useless, as were the loud protests of Suwali Woman. In a short time, the Suwalis had themselves two bound captives, and they all resumed their march.

"I think that Suwali Woman was defending us," said Cuts-Off-Their-Heads.

"Perhaps she'll defend us to our deaths," said Edohi.

Then a Suwali man carrying a spear struck Edohi across the back with his weapon and growled some kind of command. He spoke in Suwali, so Edohi did not understand the words. He took the meaning, though, to be that he should keep his mouth shut, and so he did. They marched on. The day had become hot and dry. Up ahead, Edohi could see and hear Suwali Woman talking with her brother. They appeared to be arguing with each other. Cuts-Off-Their-Heads was right, Edohi thought. She was trying to defend them, but Snake was against it. They walked on.

Then they stopped, and Edohi heard some angry Suwali voices. He looked, and just ahead he could see the charred ruins of the town he had burned. He tensed. The Suwalis grabbed their two prisoners and shoved them roughly ahead. Edohi tried to think of something to say, but before he could open his mouth to speak, someone hit him from behind and sent him sprawling into the cold ashes of his recent victory. He caught a glimpse of Cuts-Off-Their-Heads to his left. He, too, had been knocked into the ash heap.

Edohi struggled to his knees. As he turned to get up onto his feet, a Suwali man bent and scooped up ashes with his hands and flung them angrily into Edohi's face. Then he kicked Edohi in the side. Edohi doubled over, and he could not tell after that where the blows were coming from. The Suwalis beat and kicked their two prisoners almost senseless before they stopped. And then there was no respite. They were pulled back up on their feet and started on the way again.

The rest of the walk was miserable for the two bruised and battered prisoners, but eventually they came to a town.

"This is where they brought me before," Cuts-Off-Their-Heads whispered to Edohi.

They walked into the town, and men, women and children ran out to meet them with more blows and jeers. Thus they went clear through to the other side of town. Then at last the beatings stopped, and the prisoners were tied to upright poles side by side. And suddenly they were ignored by all. It was as if no one knew or cared that they were there.

"Edohi," said Cuts-Off-Their-Heads, "are you all right?"

"No bones are broken," said Edohi. "And you?"

"I'm all right. They tied me here in this same spot before, and they left me here alone all night. That's when I escaped."

"Since you escaped," said Edohi, "they probably won't leave us that way. They'll kill us tonight, or they'll watch us all night until they're ready to kill us later."

Cuts-Off-Their-Heads heaved a heavy sigh.

"Yes," he said. "You're probably right. They won't make the same mistake twice."

"Did you see where your wife went?" Edohi asked.

Cuts-Off-Their-Heads made a gesture with his head.

"That's the house of her parents," he said. "I didn't see her just now go in there. I don't know where she is. But I think she'll come to me if she gets a chance."

"I hope so," said Edohi. "She's the only chance we have of surviving this, I think."

"Yes," said Cuts-Off-Their-Heads. "I think so too."

They stood there ignored, tired and sore, for the rest of the day. The sun had crawled down to the far western rim of the Sky Vault when they saw a man walking toward them. Others followed, but they stayed several paces behind. The man stepped up to look at Cuts-Off-Their-Heads first, and his face had a look of scorn.

"So you thought you'd escaped us," he said, using the trade language.

"I did escape," said Cuts-Off-Their-Heads.

"Yes, you escaped with one of our women, but now we

have you back again, and you won't escape this time. We'll kill you soon. You and your friend."

The man then stepped over to confront Edohi. He stared threateningly at Edohi for a long quiet moment. Then he spoke again.

"And you," he said. "You are the one, they tell me, who burned our town. You're a very brave man or a very foolish one to come back here with only one companion. Did you not know that we would kill you for what you did to us?"

"I knew that you might," said Edohi.

"Yet you came anyway," said the Suwali. "Why?"

"Are you the chief of this town?" Edohi asked.

"Yes," said the man. "I'm called Lightning-Strikes-Him, and your lives are in my hands."

"Then, to answer your question," said Edohi, "I came here, knowing that I might be killed, because I want to talk to you."

"To talk to me of what?" said the chief, his head cocked slightly in a gesture of suspicious curiosity.

"I came to talk to you of peace."

"You burned my town, and now you come to talk to me of peace. Ha. There will be no talk. In the morning you will die, you and your foolish friend."

And Lightning-Strikes-Him turned sharply and strode away. Edohi had no chance to respond.

"I guess we'll die here in this place," said Cuts-Off-Their-Heads.

"Then at least," said Edohi, "we'll show these Suwalis that Real People know how to die."

"Yes," said Cuts-Off-Their-Heads. "We'll show them that, you and I."

Eighteen

THEY HAD BEEN LEFT ALONE again for some time. People in the village were still up and about, talking, eating, gathered in small clusters here and there in front of their small, conical, bark-covered houses.

"I'm hungry," said Cuts-Off-Their-Heads. "Will they at least feed us before they kill us?"

"I don't know," said Edohi. "Food is the last thing I'm thinking about."

But he did start thinking about it, and he, too, was hungry. He wished that Cuts-Off-Their-Heads had kept his mouth shut about being hungry. The thought was planted firmly in his mind, and his stomach now growled and rumbled at him. He knew that hunger was at most a minor concern, and he resented its intrusion into his thoughts. The main thing was to find a way to escape from these strange-talking Suwalis.

He would still have liked to have had a peace talk with them, but short of that, he wanted to escape with his life and with that of Cuts-Off-Their-Heads. And then there was the problem of establishing the new way back home at Ijodi.

He wondered if this trip had been a fool's mission, and he was the fool.

"You say they tied you here before?" he asked Cuts-Off-Their-Heads.

"Yes, but not like this. The time before they tied my hands up high over my head. When they all went to sleep, I climbed up the pole. We can't do that tied like this, with our hands behind our backs."

"No," said Edohi, "we can't, but we have to do something. At least, we have to try."

"If you think of anything," said Cuts-Off-Their-Heads, "let me know."

Edohi looked up just then and saw Snake walking toward them. In his right hand, Snake carried a knife.

"It may be too late already," said Edohi. "Look. Your brother-in-law is coming."

Snake stopped a few paces away from the captives. He looked from Edohi to Cuts-Off-Their-Heads. Nothing in the expression on his face gave away his feelings or his intentions.

"Have you come to kill me now, as you swore you would," said Cuts-Off-Their-Heads, "now that I'm helpless?"

Snake walked around behind Cuts-Off-Their-Heads and sliced the bonds that held him to the stake. Then he moved behind Edohi to free him.

"We're going to talk," he said. "Come with me."

.   .   .   .

Gone-in-the-Water looked to his left and up the mountainside.

"Where?" he said. "Oh, there. Yes. I see it."

He clutched at rocks and at firmly rooted plants for something to pull himself up by as he climbed toward the ginseng plant, the plant that he called *atali-guli*, the mountain climber, or *yunwi usdi*, little person. When he reached it, he looked at it closely.

"*Sagwu*," he said. "That's the first one."

He struggled on up the steep mountainside. He would have to find six more "little people" before he could pull one up for his own use. He could harvest only the seventh one. He pressed on.

"Be careful up there," he said. "You're kicking rocks down on me."

He climbed higher, and then he came to a narrow mountain trail, and the going became a bit easier. After a few steps, he stopped and sat down to rest.

"Can I help it if I've lived too long?" he said. "I'm old, and I have to stop and rest now and then."

Soon he got up and walked on, but not for long. What he was looking for would not be found along the trail. He came to a place where the continued climb up the mountainside was at least manageable, and he started to climb again. He reached for a plant to grip, and he almost pulled it up before he saw what it was.

"Ah," he said. "Excuse me, little person. You're only number two. *Tali.*"

He had to stop and rest three more times before he came across the third one. He sat down wearily beside it.

"You little people are scarce up here," he said. "Hard to find. It feels like I've been climbing this mountain all day now, and you're only number three. *Tsoi.* Where are all your brothers, little person?"

He turned his head sharply to look over his shoulder.

"What?" he said. "No, I'm not crazy. I'm not like you and Noisy. What's that? Well, I'll probably get a good answer from the little person as soon as I'll get anything from you and Noisy that makes any sense. What? You've found number four? Where? Show me."

It wasn't very far to the fourth plant, but the old man was winded again when he found it.

"Nuhgi," he said, and he sat down again to rest. It was not just that he had to catch his breath. The muscles in his legs were aching, and so were his hip joints. His right arm was tired from working with the staff on which he leaned.

"What?" he said. "Of course I'll make it. I'll find number seven. I always have before, haven't I? Come on. Let's go. I want to find it and get back home before it gets dark."

He climbed some more, and he came to a place where the mountain almost leveled off for a space before it started up again. He rested there on the flat, and he looked around, and there he found number five.

"Hisgi," he said, and he climbed again, and he found there on the steep side of the mountain, in a spot where he did not dare let go of his grip on a small tree, number six.

"Sudali."

He noted it in passing and kept climbing. For a short while he thought that he would fall. He thought that all of his strength was gone and he could not possibly hold on to anything any longer.

"Pull me up," he said. "Pull me up, or I'll fall."

He lost his staff reaching for another sapling to grasp, and he found himself somehow on top of the mountain. He was lying on his stomach on the rocky ground, panting, and when he lifted his face off the ground, he saw it there right before his eyes.

"*Galiquogi,*" he said, and he reached for it. "I'm sorry to have to take you, Mountain Climber, but I need you for my work. I need you for cures to help others. It's not for myself, little person. You're number seven. Thank you."

He pulled it out of the ground, and then he rolled over onto his back to rest, and the root that looked like a man was lying on top of his chest. His chest rose, and it fell, and it was a long interval before it rose again. It fell. There was another long space, longer than the previous one, and the chest rose again. It fell. And then the old man was still, and his shallow chest rose no more.

Snake took the two captives to one of the conical dwellings. A small fire burned in front of the house. Behind the fire, in front of the door to the house, Lightning-Strikes-Him sat on the ground cross-legged. He was lighting a long-stemmed pipe with a faggot from the fire.

"Sit down," he said, using the trade language.

Edohi glanced at Snake, and Snake indicated a spot to the left of the chief. Edohi sat down. Cuts-Off-Their-Heads was seated to Edohi's left, and Snake sat down last, across the fire from Edohi and to the right of his chief. Lightning-Strikes-Him continued to puff at his pipe. When the clouds of smoke were billowing around his head, he took the pipe out of his mouth and handed it to

Snake. Snake took four puffs and handed it to Cuts-Off-Their-Heads. Imitating his brother-in-law, Cuts-Off-Their-Heads puffed four times and passed the pipe to his right. Edohi took his four puffs and returned the pipe to its owner.

"You came to talk to us of peace," said Lightning-Strikes-Him.

"Yes," said Edohi.

"You led a party of warriors to our country. You killed many of our young men and burned one of our towns."

"Yes, I did."

"Is that a way to look for peace?"

"I attacked your town after Suwalis destroyed one of our towns. It had to be done. Things are balanced between us now. Now is the time to talk about ending this war."

"You brought with you this man who stole one of our young women," said Lightning-Strikes-Him. "I think you came here to insult us."

"I brought this man because the woman you speak of is his wife," said Edohi. "There's been a marriage between our two peoples. If we fight with each other again, these two people will be sad. They're another reason we should stop the war. That's why I brought him along."

"He stole the woman."

"But then he let her go, and she went with him willingly."

"I know that," said the chief. "I've talked with her."

He puffed on his pipe again, and again he passed it to his right. While Snake was puffing, he spoke again.

"There's another problem," he said. "When this one left here to go alone into your country, he swore to me that he would find his sister and bring her home. He swore that he would fight with the man who took her away. He swore to kill that man. He said that he would do all this, or he would not come back. He would do all this or die."

"He fought with me," said Cuts-Off-Their-Heads. "He tried to kill me, but I defeated him and captured him. I could have killed him. I would have, but I didn't want to kill my wife's brother."

"And he has come back with his sister," said Edohi. "He's done everything he swore to do."

"Everything except for killing that man," said Lightning-Strikes-Him.

The pipe came back to Edohi, and Edohi smoked.

"He brought us here and made us your prisoners," he said. "The killing is now up to you."

He handed the pipe to Lightning-Strikes-Him, and the Suwali chief held it across his legs. He stared at the flames there before him.

"Snake," he said, "get them a place to sleep. I'm going to think about all this. We'll talk again in the morning."

Snake led the two men away. He didn't speak until he came to one of the small dwellings, where he stopped and gestured toward its entry.

"You can sleep here," he said to Edohi. "Do you want a woman for the night?"

Edohi wasn't sure he had heard right.

"What?" he said.

"Do you want a woman for the night?"

"No," said Edohi. "But I'm hungry."

"Someone will bring you some food," Snake said, and

he took Cuts-Off-Their-Heads away. Edohi squatted in the entry of the house and watched, and he saw Snake lead Cuts-Off-Their-Heads to another house. There Suwali Woman came out to meet her husband, and the two of them went inside together.

Well, Edohi thought, at least it seems that we're safe until morning. In a short while an old woman came with a bowl of stew, and Edohi ate. Then he crawled inside the house and stretched himself out on the furs that were there on the ground.

A woman for the night? he thought. These Suwalis were hard people to understand. Their language sounded harsh to his ears, and their ways were equally strange. He tried to clear his mind and sleep, but he could not. He envied Cuts-Off-Their-Heads just a little, for he knew that Cuts-Off-Their-Heads would not be troubled with thoughts that night, not with Suwali Woman to keep him occupied.

Then he almost laughed at himself for that envy, for he had just turned down the offer of a Suwali woman for the night. A woman for the night. What did that mean? He drove that question out of his mind to concentrate on the more important one. What would the morning bring? Lightning-Strikes-Him had said that he would think about Edohi's proposed peace, and they would talk again in the morning. It seemed entirely possible to Edohi that the Suwali chief would think it over and decide to kill him and Cuts-Off-Their-Heads anyway.

He wondered if the smartest thing to do would be to escape. He was free. Not tied up. Not guarded as far as he could tell. But how would he get to Cuts-Off-Their-Heads without attracting the attention of others? He did not want to leave without Cuts-Off-Their-Heads. And then, if the Suwali chief meant to kill them in the morning, would he not have left them tied to the stakes all night? Why would he set them free for a talk? Why feed them and offer them women? Why give them an opportunity to escape?

He wished that he could seek the advice of his uncle Hemp Carrier, but, of course, he could not. So he asked himself, what would Hemp Carrier say? He closed his eyes, and he tried to picture his uncle there in front of him, and then he saw him.

"Edohi," said Hemp Carrier, "why did you come to the land of the Suwalis?"

"I came to talk peace with them," said Edohi.

"And what did the Suwali chief say to you?"

"He said that we'll talk further in the morning."

"So what are you wondering about? What's your question? You've got what you came for. You're having your talks."

"But, Uncle, I'm not sure that these Suwalis can be trusted."

"Did someone tell you that you could trust them when you planned this trip?"

"No."

"What did you know of the Suwalis?"

"Nothing, except that they have always been our enemies."

"So nothing has changed since you made the decision to come here and talk?"

"No," said Edohi. "Nothing's changed. Thank you, Uncle, for this talk. Thank you for coming to see me here."

Nineteen

THEY MET AGAIN, just as they had the night before, and again they smoked. This time, however, it seemed to Edohi that the town's entire population had gathered around them to watch and to listen. And this time Edohi was more relaxed than he had been the night before. He knew, of course, that the decision of Lightning-Strikes-Him could still go either way, but he felt that the talk of the night before and the passage of time had probably softened the chief's attitude toward his prisoners and toward the prospects of peace.

And there was another thing that had helped to relax Edohi. His uncle Hemp Carrier had visited him in the night. Of course, he realized that he might simply have dreamed the visit. It might not really have happened. Even so, it had seemed very real. The memory of the visit, too, was like the memory of something real. So whether it had been a dream or a real visit of some kind by his uncle, its effect on Edohi had been both calming and reassuring, and he sat across the small fire from Lightning-Strikes-Him with an attitude of something very near to arrogance. His main worry had become that he might appear to be just a little too cocky.

"I've given much thought to this matter," said Lightning-Strikes-Him. "There's much hatred here toward you Mountain People. Many of the people here in this town had relatives and friends in the town you wiped out not so long ago."

"The town your people wiped out," said Cuts-Off-Their-Heads, "was my own town, yet I married one of your women, and I came here with Edohi to try to establish peace between our people."

"Yes," said the chief. "I know that, and I've thought about that, too. I've thought about everything."

His pipe had gone out, and he calmly refilled and relit it. Everyone else waited in the silence that he had established and that he alone for the moment commanded. When he had his pipe going again, he again passed it around, and he maintained the silence until it had come back to him. He laid the pipe across his thighs, and he heaved a heavy sigh. Then he spoke.

"We will end this war," he said, "and you three will go back to your homes in safety. But first we will celebrate the new peace."

The celebration lasted for four days. There was feasting which bordered on gluttony, and there were singing and dancing and much boastful oratory. Edohi found the manner of the celebration very strange, the songs harsh and discordant, the dancing frenetic, but by the end of the four days, he felt as if he had made a number of new friends. The Suwali acceptance of the peace seemed to be genuine, and Edohi had no reason to doubt that it would last.

On the morning after the last day of the celebration, Edohi, Cuts-Off-Their-Heads and Suwali Woman, accompanied by four Suwali warriors and Lightning-Strikes-Him, started for home. The Suwalis were going along for a very specific reason. They would not consider the peace to be formally established until they, too, had been feasted and entertained in the other party's home. Thus far, the Suwalis had merely dealt with two individuals, and that was not enough. It was a long journey back, but an uneventful one, and everyone was greeted warmly upon their arrival back at Ijodi.

Because the people of Ijodi had understood the purpose of Edohi's trip, they were not surprised to see him return in the company of Suwalis, nor were they hostile to the Suwalis who entered their town. They greeted them as new friends. But Edohi had a problem. Since the new way was yet to be established, there was no formal structure in place, and Lightning-Strikes-Him was expecting some kind of formal response to his own formalities. Edohi needed some sound advice.

As soon as he could get away from his Suwali guests, Edohi went to the home of Gone-in-the-Water just outside the walls of the town. The old man was not outside, so Edohi stepped up under the arbor.

"Uncle," he called out. "Are you home? It's Edohi come to see you."

There was no answer. He stepped tentatively to the door of the small house and bent to look inside. There were no windows in the house, just the small doorway, and even it was shaded by the arbor. There was no fire, inside or out, and so the interior was dark, even in the daylight. Edohi waited a moment for his eyes to adjust to the darkness, and then he saw the old conjurer. He was laid out on the cot against the wall to Edohi's left. He was not moving. The stillness around suddenly seemed to Edohi to become overwhelming.

"Uncle?" he said.

There was no response. He stepped inside and moved slowly and cautiously, as if he were afraid he might awaken the conjurer or step on something fragile and break it, to the cot where the old man lay. He looked closely, and he saw no movement of the chest or stomach. He leaned over the wrinkled old face, and he heard no sound of breathing, felt no movement of air. He laid a hand on the body and found it cold to his touch. The old man was dead. Lying on his chest was the man-shaped root of a mountain climber plant.

Preparations for the funeral took a day, and they waited another four days for the final visit of the old man's spirit before its departure to the Ghost Country in the Darkening Land. Then they burned his house. They left his tiny old body wrapped in a bear's hide lying on a scaffold not far from where his house had been. Later the bones would be cleaned and buried.

But the five days' delay gave Edohi the time he needed to make preparations for the other business. He was not directly involved in the funeral preparations or rites, and so he took advantage of the time to pay another visit to Dancing Rabbit in Kituwah.

"I made the peace with the Suwalis," he said, "but

they've come home with me. We need to do something formal with them in Ijodi to conclude the peace. Some kind of ceremony is needed. Can you help me with this? Do you know of something?"

"Yes," said Dancing Rabbit. "There is something I remember, but we have to have someone in a position of authority. We have to do the other thing first. Select our chiefs and councils. You know."

"That will take some time, and the Suwalis are already delayed for five days by the funeral of the old conjurer at Ijodi."

Edohi was not speaking disrespectfully of the old man. He was simply avoiding the use of the dead man's name.

"I don't know what we can do without someone who has an official position," said Dancing Rabbit.

"Well then," said Edohi, "tell me about the ceremony. Then I'll go back to Ijodi and see if I can delay the Suwalis long enough to do all of these things."

Edohi was surprised to find that Lightning-Strikes-Him was in no hurry to return to his own home. In the short time he had been in Ijodi he had gotten acquainted with Corn Sifter. She was a longtime widow, and apparently she had entertained a good many men over the years. The Suwali chief discovered that, though the Real People did not have actual prostitutes the way his own people did, there were some women who chose a role very close to that for themselves. Among the Real People, he found, women, especially unmarried women, made almost all of their own decisions. He found that just a little strange.

As for Corn Sifter, she found the dalliance with the Suwali chief both pleasant and amusing, but she knew that even if he should ask her to leave with him when the time came for him to depart, she would not. She had heard of the different way the Suwalis treated their women, and she had no desire to lower her status. But for a few days, he would be fun.

So Edohi's worries about the timing proved to be of no significance. Lightning-Strikes-Him was happy to stretch out his visit to his former enemies. It was a good thing, too, for the original plan had been to hold the town meeting on the fourth day following Edohi's return from the Suwali country. Gone-in-the-Water's funeral had precluded that, and it did not seem to Edohi to be good form to have the meeting immediately after the funeral. It was moved back another four days. Again, Edohi put the extra days to good use.

At the suggestion of Edohi, Wild Hemp, Hemp Carrier, the Spoiler and others, even the Shawnee, talked to everyone they could about the new way. They said that there should be two chiefs, a war chief and a peace chief. They said that the war chief should be the one to deal with outsiders. If there was a war to be fought, he would be in charge. If there was a peace to be concluded, he should be in charge of that, too. If the people of Ijodi wanted to establish trading relations with some foreign people, the war chief would be the one to deal with that issue. In short, he would be in charge of any and all relationships of the Real People of Ijodi with any and all outsiders.

The peace chief, they said, would be the authority at home. He would determine when the ceremonies should be held, and he would preside over them. He would also preside over any domestic disputes which might arise.

And they talked further. They said that they did not believe that anyone, no, not any two men, should have so much power to themselves. That was the reason they had killed the *Ani-Kutani*. Each of these two chiefs, they said, should have a council of seven to help them arrive at major decisions. These councilmen should be selected by the women of the seven clans, one from each clan for each council.

"But once these sixteen men are in power," someone asked, "what would prevent them from becoming as overbearing as did the *Ani-Kutani?* Sixteen is not so many. There were more than sixteen priests."

But the priests were the authority over all of the towns of the Real People, the advocates of the new way answered. These sixteen men, two chiefs, each with a seven-man council, will be the authority only over Ijodi. If the other towns see the wisdom of this new way, then each town will have its sixteen men.

But the real authority, they said, for Edohi had coached them well, will be with the people. If the women of a clan appoint a man to represent them on one of the councils and he turns out to be lazy or incompetent or abusive, if he fails to perform his duties in a satisfactory manner, then those same women can recall him from that position and appoint another to serve in his place.

"And the chiefs?" some asked. "How will they be selected? There are seven clans and only two chiefs."

The first time, to get the new way established, by the voice of all, the whole population of the town. In the future they will be kept in office or replaced if need be by their own councils.

"You mean the chiefs are not in command of the councils?"

No. The councils are over the chiefs. The councils will make the decisions, and then the chiefs will be charged with carrying out those decisions.

"But the women are in control of the councilmen. They select them, and they can call them back."

Yes. So the clans are in control. Our sisters, our wives and our mothers.

And everyone in Ijodi talked about the new way. And most of the talk was in its favor. There was no real opposition. Those not yet enthusiastic about the idea were merely asking questions and mulling it over. No one was arguing against it.

And Edohi's supporters did not openly promote Edohi for the position of war chief. They let others do that for them, and others did. It was a natural thing to do. Edohi had led them into two major victories, and now he had concluded a peace with a longtime enemy. He had three times proven his abilities in the two major areas of service of the war chief as the position was being defined. What other choice could there be?

Hemp Carrier helped to start all the talk, and then he held back to listen. He heard others promoting the ideas he had started to spread. He listened to others extol the virtues of his nephew Edohi and call for Edohi to be put forward as war chief. He even heard some arguments regarding who should have the honor of nominating Edohi for this position. Hemp Carrier felt proud and pleased, even a little smug.

Several names were mentioned as possibilities for the role of peace chief, but no one name surfaced as stronger than the others. There would be more debate on this one, Hemp Carrier could see. The debate would likely continue into the formal meeting and even drag the meeting out longer than might be desirable. But it couldn't be helped. He himself could not even come up with the name of a man he thought best suited to that position. He considered several names, but none stood out. He had questions about all of them. Well, something would work out at the meeting. The people would decide on someone. The main thing was that they were convinced that the new way as it had been proposed by Edohi was the best thing to do. Almost as good was the fact that they seemed also to be convinced that Edohi was the only man to fill the role of war chief.

Twenty

THE WHOLE TOWN of Ijodi showed up for the big meeting. There were even visitors from Kituwah and a few from more remote towns. The visitors had heard of what the people of Ijodi were up to, and they were curious to find out how things would turn out. Some were already talking about doing the same thing in their own towns, talking about adopting this new way for themselves. Edohi, of course, heard some of the talk, and he was well pleased. His highest hope was just exactly that— that his new way would spread throughout the country of the Real People, and that every town would have its own government of two chiefs, each with a seven-member council. That goal was yet a long way off, he knew, but the early reactions from the visitors were certainly promising.

Then, just as everyone expected, Edohi was named as the only candidate for the role of war chief, and not a voice was raised in opposition. And so he was proclaimed to be the new war chief, and it was still early in the meeting. That done, the next task was to select a peace chief. Several names were thrown out for consideration, and there followed much heated debate. One of the names was that of Agili, brother of the Spoiler.

As the debate continued, one name after another fell by the wayside, as supporters of certain candidates simply quit speaking out. They saw that they were outnumbered, or they had become convinced by others, or they just grew weary of the debate. At last no one was speaking up for anyone except Agili, and Agili, therefore, became the peace chief.

The meeting was over, and it was still early in the afternoon. It was time for the clan women to meet among themselves and select the men who would make up the two councils. They would gather at once and meet, clear into the night if need be, to make their decisions, and the general population would gather again the next day to hear the choices.

Lightning-Strikes-Him found the entire proceeding fascinating until he returned to the house he had been using and found out that Corn Sifter had gone to the meeting of her clan women. There was nothing else for him to do, so he began to stroll around the town with his fellow tribesmen.

In front of the townhouse, some men were playing the *gatayusti* game, rolling the stone wheel and throwing the spear after it. Other men were placing bets on the outcome of the game. Dancing Rabbit was there with his nephew, Gnat, watching. He noticed the arrival of the Suwalis with interest, and a new thought came into his mind. He wondered at himself that he had not thought of it sooner. It was so simple and so obvious.

"Gnat," he said.

"Yes, Uncle?"

"The Real People have been at war with the Suwalis for as long as any of us can remember."

"Yes," said Gnat. "Certainly for a longer time than I can recall."

"The Real People and the Suwalis have never traded with one another," said Dancing Rabbit. "Never."

"Are you thinking that we should trade with the Suwalis?" asked the boy, his eyes widening with interest and anticipated adventure.

"Maybe," said Dancing Rabbit. "Maybe. It would be a much easier way to start our new venture than by going so far south as I had been thinking before. These Suwalis don't live so very far away from us. And it looks like we're going to have a new peace with them. It would be good, I think, to be the first traders to take advantage of this new peace. We'll see what happens."

Edohi could scarcely believe how smoothly everything was going. He had anticipated long debates, arguments, serious objections to his proposed new way, but there had been none. Perhaps the people were so desperate for some order in their lives that they simply agreed to the first idea that was proposed to them. Or maybe Hemp Carrier and the others had done their jobs extremely well, persuading the others of the advisability of the new way in advance of the meeting. Whatever the reason, it looked to Edohi as if things were going to work out exactly according to his plans.

He thought about old Gone-in-the-Water and the advice he had given. He knew, too, that the old conjurer had done even more. He had performed certain rituals to ensure the success of Edohi and the new way. He wished for a moment that the old man had lived long enough to see this outcome, and then he asked himself if maybe Gone-in-the-Water wasn't watching from someplace anyway.

He probably is watching, he thought. He was a very powerful man, that one. I'll miss him a great deal.

It was early afternoon of the next day when the clan women finally called for the next meeting of the whole town, and when the people had all gathered to hear, they announced the names of the seven men who would form the council of the war chief and the seven who would form the peace chief's council. Edohi was well pleased, and the general population approved of the action. It was done. The new way was in place.

They gathered in the townhouse around a small fire. Edohi sat across from Lightning-Strikes-Him. Behind Edohi sat his seven councilors, and behind the Suwali chief sat the four Suwali warriors who had accompanied him to Ijodi. Edohi sprinkled bits of cedar in the fire and wafted the smoke over himself and his honored guest with the feather of an eagle. He filled with ancient tobacco the bowl of a clay pipe which bore the carved head of an eagle, and he lit the tobacco with the smoldering end of a faggot from the fire. He puffed four times and passed the pipe to Lightning-Strikes-Him. All of these things he did according to instructions he had received from Dancing Rabbit.

"From this day forth," he said, "the Suwalis are the friends of the Real People of Ijodi. The ancient war between our two peoples is at an end. The enemies of the Suwalis will be our enemies, and their friends will be our friends."

Then the speech was repeated in the trade language for the benefit of Lightning-Strikes-Him, and the Suwali chief spoke in response, using his own tongue. One of the Suwali warriors standing behind him repeated his words in the jargon.

"I am happy about this new peace between our peoples," he said. "Your enemies are our enemies, and your friends are our friends. Any of our people who kills one of yours or who steals from you will be an outcast. The old war is no more."

For four days then they feasted, and at night they danced and sang. And Lightning-Strikes-Him, in his free time, dallied more with the widow Corn Sifter. And Edohi went to the house of his new wife, Sohi.

"Is everything going well?" she asked him.

"Yes," he said. "I'm well pleased at the outcome of the meeting. I don't care so much about being war chief, but the people want me, so it seems I must."

"This is what you were born to do," said Sohi. "Are you hungry?"

"No," said Edohi. "We've been doing nothing but eating, it seems to me. I have some time now to spend with you alone. I've been away from you too much. I haven't been a good husband to you, I think."

"I haven't complained," she said.

"No," said Edohi. "You haven't. You're much too good for that."

Edohi stretched himself out on the floor, leaning up on one elbow. Sohi knelt down beside him. Edohi reached out and ran his fingers through her long hair.

"You're a beautiful woman, Sohi," he said, "and I'm a very fortunate man to have you for my wife."

"Do you mean that, Edohi?" she said.

His arm went around her shoulders, and he pulled her over on top of him.

"Yes," he said. "I mean what I say, and from now on, I mean to spend as much of my time with you as I can."

Their arms went around each other, and the two bodies rolled together on the thick black bearskin rug which covered the ground there in the house of Sohi.

At last the four-day celebration came to an end, and Lightning-Strikes-Him and his Suwali companions prepared to leave Ijodi. Dancing Rabbit paid a hurried visit to Edohi.

"As war chief," he said, "you're in charge of trade negotiations with other people. I've come to ask if I may begin my life as a trader by taking my wares to the Suwalis, our new allies."

"Of course," said Edohi. "We wouldn't have a peace without the advice you gave me. Besides, what better way to reinforce our new alliance with Lightning-Strikes-Him than by a trading mission? Will you take your nephew along?"

"Yes, and I'd like to go now."

"Now would be a good time," said Edohi. "You can

travel with Lightning-Strikes-Him. Let's go to see him now before he leaves."

The Suwali chief was delighted with the prospect of taking home with him a trader from the Real People. His own people would be well enough impressed with him because of the peace, but when they saw that a trader had come back with him, they would be even better pleased, even more impressed with his diplomacy and statesmanship.

"Yes," he said loudly. "Come back with me and bring all your wares. My people will all want to trade with our new friends."

Many of the people of Ijodi followed the travelers outside the walls of the town and watched them as they began their journey. They waved and shouted farewells as long as the two groups could see and hear each other.

Standing to one side with her husband the Shawnee, the Spoiler watched, a contented smile on her face. They had come through hard times, all of them, but everything had worked out after all for the best. Her second daughter was married to Edohi, and Edohi was now a chief. The other chief was her brother. And of course, as did everyone else, she had two clansmen on the councils. Edohi had done very well with this new way, she thought. It should work well for the Real People. She put an arm around the waist of her husband.

"So," she said, "what do you think now of your adopted people, my Shawnee?"

"I think," he said, "that this should be a very good place in which to raise our son."

Glossary

Cherokee words, phrases and names used in *The White Path*

Agehyuh woman.

Agili masculine name, He-Is-Rising.

Ani-Chahta Choctaws, or Choctaw People; *ani*, plural prefix + *Chahta*, Choctaw.

Ani-chuja the boys, Cherokee name for the Pleiades.

Ani-Cusa Muskogee or Creek People; *ani*, plural prefix + *Cusa*, Creeks.

Ani-Kutani *ani*, plural prefix + *Kutani*, a priest. An ancient Cherokee priesthood. Plural form. The exact meaning of the word cannot be determined. The *Ani-Kutani* were overthrown in *The Dark Way*.

Ani-Suwali Suwali people or Suwalis; *ani*, plural prefix + *Suwali*, the Cherokee designation of a southeastern Siouan tribe usually called Cheraw.

Ani-yunwi-ya the Real People, Cherokee designation for themselves; *ani*, plural prefix + *yunwi* (person) + *ya* (real or original).

Atali-guli ginseng, literally, mountain climber. Also called *yunwi-usdi* or little person.

Edohi masculine Cherokee name, He-Is-Wandering-About or He-Is-Walking.

Galiquogi seven, a powerful sacred number.

Gatayusti a gambling game played with a stone disc and a spear, common to most southeastern Indians, called Chunkey by the Creeks.

Gili-utsuhstanuhyi Where-the-Dog-Ran, Cherokee name for the Milky Way.

Ha an exclamation.

Hisgi five.

Ijodi alternate spellings, Itsodi, Echota. An ancient Cherokee town. The meaning of the word is lost.

Iya pumpkin.

Iya-Iyusti Iya + iyusti (like), hence, Like-a-Pumpkin, a masculine name.

Iyusti like or similar.

Jola tobacco.

Jola gayunli ancient (or sacred) tobacco.

Kituwah alternate spelling, Keetoowah, an ancient Cherokee town, perhaps the "Mother Town" of the Cherokees. *Ani-Keetoowah* or Keetoowah People is another way in which Cherokees have referred to themselves over the years.

Kutani a priest; see *Ani-Kutani* above.

Nuhgi four, a sacred number.

Osi winter house or hot house, also used as a sweat house. A small dome-shaped structure beside the main house.

Sagwu one.

Sawahani Shawnee.

'Siyo contracted form of *osiyo*, a greeting.

Sohi hickory nut; in the story, Hickory Nut, a feminine name.

Sudali six.

Tali two.

Taskigi ancient Cherokee town name; meaning cannot be deciphered.

Tohiju how are you?

Tsoi three.

Tsundigewi a mythic tribe of little people.

Uk'ten' contraction of *ukitena* (keen-eyed), mythical creature in Cherokee lore. He's like a giant rattlesnake but with horns and wings.

Wado thank you.

Yunwi-usdi little person (*yunwi*, person; *usdi*, little); a name for the ginseng plant (see *atali-guli* above).